Eva and the Hidden Diary

JUDI CURTIN grew up in Cork and now lives in Limerick where she is married with three children. Judi is the author of *Eva's Journey*, *Eva's Holiday* and *Leave it to Eva* as well as the best-selling 'Alice & Megan' series. With Roisin Meaney, she is the author of *See If I Care*. She has also written three novels, *Sorry, Walter*, *From Claire to Here* and *Almost Perfect*. Her books have sold into Serbian, Portuguese, German, Russian, Lithuanian and most recently to Australia and New Zealand.

The 'Alice & Megan' series

Alice Next Door
Alice Again
Don't Ask Alice
Alice in the Middle
Bonjour Alice
Alice & Megan Forever
Alice to the Rescue
Alice & Megan's Cookbook

The 'Eva' Series

Eva's Journey
Eva's Holiday
Leave it to Eva

Other Books

See If I Care (with Roisin Meaney)

Judi Curtin

THE O'BRIEN PRESS
DUBLIN

First published 2013 by The O'Brien Press Ltd,
12 Terenure Road East, Rathgar, Dublin 6, Ireland.
Tel: +353 1 4923333; Fax: +353 1 4922777
E-mail: books@obrien.ie
Website: www.obrien.ie

ISBN: 978-1-84717-588-5

1 2 3 4 5 6 7 8
13 14 15 16

Layout and design: The O'Brien Press Ltd
Cover illustration: Woody Fox
Printed and bound by CPI Group (UK) Ltd, Croydon, CR0 4YY
The paper used in this book is produced using pulp from managed forests

The O'Brien Press receives assistance from

Chapter One

I was nervous as I walked towards the front door. After all, I was the one who'd brought this family together, and if they were unhappy, it would be partly my fault.

I took a deep breath and knocked. There was no answer. They probably couldn't hear me above the sudden burst of laughter that came from inside. I took a step closer and peeped through the open door. Inside, my friend Kate and her step-mum Zoe were doubled over laughing like they were going to die. Kate's Dad, Patrick, and her little brother, Simon, were rolling on the floor, having some kind of noisy play-fight that involved lots of stuffed toys and cushions and armfuls of shredded newspaper. In the corner, Kate's granny, Martha, was calmly knitting, as if nothing much was going on.

I knew it was rude, but I stood there for a while and watched. I remembered when I'd first met Kate. Back then she'd lived with Martha, while Patrick, Zoe and Simon lived in London. Kate was lonely and sad, and in the end, I stepped in and managed to get the family back together. When they appeared, Kate's worst summer magically turned into her best summer ever.

I was wondering if I should just walk away, leaving them to their happy family stuff, when Kate looked up and saw me.

'OMG!' she squealed. 'You're here. At last you're here! Hey, everyone, Eva's here.'

I stepped inside, and they all said 'hi' (except for Simon, who was busy attacking his dad's leg with a furry dinosaur). I couldn't answer though, as Kate had raced towards me and almost knocked me to the ground in a great big bear hug.

'I'm guessing you missed me too,' I said when I finally escaped.

'A small bit,' she said, looking embarrassed.

It was great to see her again. Kate lives in Seacove, and my family only goes there for the holidays. The rest of the year Kate and I communicate by text and phone and Skype. It helps, but it's not the same as being together.

Kate wiped the tears of laughter from her eyes. 'Beach?' she said.

I nodded. I felt all warm and excited as we waved goodbye and set off for the beach. Three whole weeks in Seacove! I knew it was going to be amazing.

'Why did Lily have to go on holidays *this* week, of all weeks,' I said, as soon as we were settled in our favourite spot on the beach. 'I'm dying to see her. When does she get back?'

'Not for another week and a bit,' said Kate. 'And even then we probably won't see much of her. Her mum's catering business has got really busy, so Lily has to help her most days.'

'So what have you been doing with yourself?'

She shrugged. 'Mostly just hanging out with the family. Dad and I go for walks and stuff. Sometimes I stay home and play with Zoe and Simon. It's not very exciting, but I like it.'

I smiled to myself as I lay back on the sand. I felt a special responsibility for the whole family, and was glad to see that things were working out OK.

'So it's all happy-ever-after around here these days?' I said.

'Yeah, kind of, but ...'

I sat up again quickly. 'But what?' I asked. 'Happy-ever-afters don't end with buts. What's wrong, Kate?'

She smiled a forced kind of smile. 'It's nothing,' she said. 'I'm probably just being stupid.'

I put my face right up next to hers. 'Tell me,' I said. 'Tell me what's wrong.'

She sighed. 'You're not going to give up, are you?'

I shook my head. 'Never. You might as well tell me now, before I drag it out of you.'

'It's Zoe,' she said.

I couldn't believe what I was hearing.

'*Zoe!*' I said. 'But Zoe is lovely. She's always been really nice to you. Just tell me what she's done and I'll sort her out for you. I'm not afraid of her. I could easily—'

Kate giggled and I was glad to see that she hadn't lost her sense of humour in the time we'd been apart.

'Zoe is still lovely,' she said. 'That hasn't changed. She's the best. She's smart and funny and kind. She always backs me up when Dad's being an idiot.'

I giggled. 'What is it about dads? Mine's great, but sometimes he drives me totally crazy.'

Kate laughed too. 'Tell me about it,' she said. 'Luckily, Zoe always defends me when Dad's going ballistic about stupid stuff. It's really cool the way she's always on my side.'

'That's great, but I don't get it. I thought you said there was a problem with Zoe?'

'Well, she loves spending time with Dad and me and Simon, and when Martha's bones are hurting, and she's in a bad mood, Zoe is the best at making her come around—'

'I'm still not seeing the problem here.'

Kate gave a big sigh. 'Sometimes I think Zoe might be bored. She hasn't made any friends in Seacove. She never says so exactly, but I can tell that she misses London. She misses her job.'

'That's kind of normal, though, isn't it?'

'Yeah – of course it is. Oh, Eva! I love Zoe and I really want her to be happy. But what if she can't be happy here with us in Seacove? What if she needs to be in London to be happy?'

I was still figuring out how to answer that, when she continued.

'And there's another thing too.'

'What?'

'Zoe coming here was always only supposed to be a temporary arrangement, remember? Zoe and Dad only came to help out while Martha was sick – and Martha's better now. What if they decide to go back to London? What will I do then?'

I hugged her. 'Try not to worry,' I said. 'It'll be fine. I'm sure of it.'

I wasn't sure of it at all, so I couldn't meet Kate's eyes when she smiled back at me.

'You're right,' she said. 'I'm just being stupid. I'm worrying about nothing. And besides ...'

'Besides what?'

'Besides, when you're around everything always gets better. Now that you're here, Zoe will see what a totally exciting place Seacove can be. All I've got to do is sit back and wait for you to work your magic.'

'So no pressure then?'

She giggled. 'No, Eva. No pressure at all.'

Chapter Two

Next morning, we were still having breakfast when Kate called over. She said 'hi' to Mum and Dad, and gave Joey a huge hug. He pretended to be embarrassed, but I knew he was pleased. He really likes Kate.

'How's your mum?' she asked him.

Joey's mum, Monica, owns the cottage we stay in. She often has to go to hospital, and that's why Joey usually comes on holidays with us. He's really cute and is kind of like the little brother I never had.

'Mum's OK,' he said. 'Her last operation was a big success.'

'I'm glad,' she said. She stepped forward to

give him another hug, but he ducked away. I guess little boys can only cope with the occasional hug.

Kate turned to me. 'What do you want to do for the day, Eva?' she asked. 'We could go back to the beach again, or we could go see Jeremy if you like.'

Believe it or not, Jeremy's not a person or a pet – it's a tree! One that's very special to Kate. One summer, a developer wanted to chop it down, but, with the help of the locals and some tourists, Kate and I had managed to save it.

Kate was grinning at me, and I thought back to when I first met her. In the beginning, I thought she was totally weird and when I heard that she actually called a tree by a boy's name I decided she was completely crazy. That was all a long time ago though. (Now, I couldn't help thinking that Jeremy was an especially good name for a tree.)

'So make up your mind,' said Kate,

interrupting my thoughts. 'Beach or Jeremy? The suspense is killing me.'

Before I could decide what to do though, Mum stepped in.

'Not so fast, Eva,' she said. 'Remember you promised Monica that you'd clean out the old shed in the back garden? Since she's nice enough to let us stay here, the least we can do is help out with some odd jobs while we're here.'

I groaned. 'I know I promised Monica, Mum,' I said. 'And I *will* clean the shed. But do I have to do it right now?'

Mum folded her arms, a dangerous warning sign. I wondered if it was worth having a row – especially as Mum was sure to win. (It's easy to win rows when you've got all the money and all the power and can do totally mean stuff like banning sweets and confiscating mobile phones.)

'I'll help you, if you like,' said Kate suddenly. 'It'll be fun.'

'Fun?' I made a face at her. 'If cleaning out dirty old sheds is your idea of fun, maybe you need to get out more.'

Kate made a face back at me. 'Maybe we'll find some ancient treasures,' she said.

'I very much doubt that,' said Mum, handing me a roll of black rubbish bags. 'I expect that shed is full of junk. I peeped in last night, and it looks like no one's stepped inside there for many years. Just pack everything into these bags, and we can leave them out for the bin men to take away.'

I took the bags and followed Kate out to the back garden. I wasn't happy to be wasting a precious morning in a stinky old shed.

'Let's just get this over with as fast as possible,' I said. 'And then I can get on with my holiday.'

I slid back the rusty bolt and pulled the shed door towards me. It opened with a horrible screechy scratchy sound.

Kate grinned. 'That's the ghost of the shed

welcoming us,' she said. 'If we're not careful, it will haunt us for the rest of the summer.'

Even though it was a lovely sunny day, I suddenly felt cold. I don't like thinking about ghosts and creepy stuff like that.

The shed was quite small, and it had shelves all along one side. There was a window on the back wall, but it was cracked and dirty and hardly let in any light.

I stepped inside and picked up a cardboard box, which immediately fell apart in my hands. I jumped as heaps of rusty old nails and screws clattered to the ground and rolled into the dark, cobwebby corners of the shed.

'Brilliant,' I muttered. 'A great start.'

Kate didn't answer as she was already on her knees filling the first rubbish bag. I gave a big sigh, and then I rolled up my sleeves and began to help her.

Hours later, Kate and I were almost finished. We'd filled up ten rubbish bags, and apart from an ugly old china vase, we hadn't found anything worth keeping.

'Here, this is the last thing,' I said, as I reached into the furthest, darkest corner of the shed to pick up an old biscuit tin that was almost covered by layers of dust and cobwebs.

'Maybe there's treasure inside that tin,' said Kate. 'Maybe it's a secret stash of gold and silver and diamonds and pearls. Maybe we're going to be rich!'

I grinned. 'If it was treasure, it would belong to Monica – not that it matters. This tin is probably full of useless junk, just like everything else we've found in this dump.'

'You've got no imagination, Eva,' said Kate. 'I bet there's something amazing inside. Bring it out onto the grass, so we can have a proper look.'

I did what she said. It was nice to be back in

the sunshine again. The two of us sat on the grass and looked at the box for a minute.

'This is so amazing,' said Kate. 'It's like going back in time. I bet no one has seen or touched this box for years and years and years.'

She was probably right. The corners of the box were all rusty, and the flowers on the lid were dull and faded.

A cloud came over the sun and I shivered.

'Let's get this over with so we can go see Jeremy,' I said.

Kate held the bottom of the box, while I used both hands to lift the lid off. Flakes of rust blew away in the breeze as the lid came free. Suddenly I couldn't help feeling a little flutter of excitement. Maybe there was going to be something amazing inside after all.

'Oh,' I said, disappointed, as I saw the rolled up piece of white material inside. 'It's only a dirty old rag.'

I reached in and took out the fabric. As I did

so, something tumbled out of it and onto the ground next to me.

I picked it up, half afraid that it was going to fall apart in my hands.

'What is it?' said Kate impatiently.

It was a grubby old leather-covered book.

'It's just ...' I said, and then I stopped talking as I turned the book over in my hands, and read what it said on the cover.

'OMG!' I said. 'It's a diary. We've found someone's ancient old diary.'

Chapter Three

I was about to open the first page of the diary, when Kate put her hand on mine.

'Stop, Eva,' she said. 'That's a diary. You can't read it.'

'Why not?' I asked.

'Because diaries are meant to be private. I'd die if you ever read mine.'

'You've got a diary? You never said.'

Now she went red. 'Well, I'm glad I never told you, if you think it would be OK to read it.'

'Of course I wouldn't read *your* diary,' I said. 'You're my friend, and that would be weird, but this is different. This diary is really, really old.

It's like a historical artifact. And we have no idea who it belongs to. Whoever wrote it must be ancient now – if they're even still alive.'

'Maybe it belongs to Monica's granny or granddad.'

I shook my head. 'No, it couldn't be anything to do with Monica. She only bought this house a few years ago.'

'Of course,' said Kate. 'I forgot that.'

'Anyway,' I said, reaching for the cover of the diary again. 'There's only one way to find out who owns it.'

Kate put her hand out again, as if she wanted to stop me, and then she pulled away. She was trying not to show it, but I could see that she was interested too.

I opened the first page, and gasped. The handwriting was beautiful, all fancy curves and loops. It was dull and faded, but I could still read what it said.

This is the Diary of Daisy Bridget Lavelle
June 6th 1947

'OMG,' I gasped. 'It's totally ancient. It's like something out of a history book.'

'It's still someone's private diary,' said Kate primly.

I ignored her. 'It's so cool,' I said. 'I wonder who Daisy Lavelle was. I wonder what she was like. I wonder if she's alive. I wonder if she still lives around here.'

Kate shook her head. 'There aren't any Lavelles here. I've never even heard the name before.'

I caught the corner of the page, ready to turn it over. Kate was staring at me, like I was about to commit a terrible crime.

'One page,' I said. 'One page and then I'll

stop reading.'

Kate didn't reply, so I quickly turned the page and saw more of the same elaborate handwriting. As I read the words aloud, I tried to picture the girl who had written them, so many years before.

Dear Diary,

My thirteenth birthday is nearly over. I have had such a lovely day. My friend Rose gave me a beautiful handkerchief, which she embroidered herself. After dinner, little Martha came across the lane with a bunch of wild flowers for me. She is a darling girl. If I had a little sister, I would like one exactly like her.

'OMG,' said Kate. 'Little Martha. That must be my granny. I love her to bits, but somehow I can't imagine her as a sweet little girl.'

I giggled. 'Me neither. That's totally weird.'

As Kate was distracted by thinking about a sweet young Martha, I turned another page. I was disappointed to see that Daisy's birthday entry only had a few more words. I read them aloud.

Mammy and Daddy gave me this diary, which is the nicest thing I have ever in my life owned. I am going to write in it every single night. Good night.

'Happy now?' asked Kate.

I shook my head. 'Not really. It's kind of disappointing. I don't think poor old Daisy has much to say for herself.'

'Yeah, well, it's probably not her fault. I'm guessing thirteen-year-olds in the 1940s had kind of boring lives.'

'That's for sure,' I said. 'It doesn't sound like Daisy had the most exciting birthday ever, does it? What was your thirteenth birthday like, Kate? I hope it was more exciting than hers.'

'My thirteenth birthday was before Dad and Zoe and Simon came back,' said Kate. 'Martha did her best – she bought me a new tracksuit, and she made me a big chocolate cake, but ...'

'But what?' I helped her.

'But it was kind of lonely. Dad forgot to send a card, and that made me feel really, really bad.'

'You poor thing,' I said, starting to feel sorry that I'd brought the subject up.

But Kate just grinned. 'Ancient history,' she said. 'What about you, Eva? Tell me about your birthdays.'

'My twelfth birthday was totally amazing,' I sighed. 'My friends and I had a pamper day in a big fancy hotel. We went swimming, and had our hair and our nails done. Then we went for pizza and I had the biggest, sparkliest cake I'd ever seen. Everyone said it was the best party they'd ever, ever been to. Only thing is ...'

'What?' asked Kate.

'I feel kind of guilty about all the stuff I used to have. I had more toys than I could play with, and more clothes than I could ever, ever wear.

Back then, I thought I needed all that stuff, and now I feel bad. Think of poor Daisy – she was happy, even though her only presents were a home-made hanky, a diary and a bunch of wild flowers.'

'And what about your thirteenth birthday?' asked Kate. 'What was that like?'

I sighed. 'By the time my thirteenth birthday came around, I was older and wiser and poorer. Mum and Dad had lost their jobs, and we'd sold our big house.'

'Poor you,' said Kate.

'It wasn't so bad,' I said, trying not to think of Kate spending her birthday all alone with Martha. 'I'd moved to a new school, and made lots of new friends. It was a good birthday, really.'

I looked down at the diary in my hands. I was dying to read more, but the way Kate was looking at me made me feel bad.

I carefully wrapped the diary in the white

fabric and stood up.

'What are you going to do with it?' asked Kate. 'You can't put it back in the shed.'

'I'm going to put it inside where it's safe,' I said. 'Just in case old Daisy Lavelle comes knocking on the door tonight, looking for it.'

Kate giggled. I ran inside and put the diary on the dresser in the corner of my bedroom, and then went back outside to join my friend.

Chapter Four

That night, Mum, Dad and I played Monopoly with Joey. As usual, Dad kept robbing the bank when he thought no one was looking, and then acting all hurt when Mum accused him of cheating. Joey laughed, because he's just a kid, but for me the whole thing was totally, totally boring. In the end, I deliberately lost, and decided to go to bed early. I was tucked up in bed and just reaching for my book, when I spotted the diary.

'Maybe Daisy's ancient old secrets will send me off to sleep,' I thought, as I opened the diary and began to read.

Dear Diary,

I felt a bit blue this morning, as it's not my birthday any more. I have to wait a whole 364 days for another one to come along. I wonder what will happen this year. I wonder will any of my dreams come true.

Daisy was describing exactly how I feel on the day after my birthday! Maybe this long-ago girl and I weren't so different after all. I couldn't help smiling to myself, which I know is a bit weird.

I turned to the next page. Some of the writing was so faded, it was hard to make it out, and by the time I got to the fourth page, I was already starting to yawn. But something made me want to keep on reading …

Much, much later Mum came into my room.

'I saw your light on, Eva,' she said. 'Why are you still awake at this hour?'

I quickly closed the diary. 'Sorry, Mum,' I said.

She kissed me and switched off the light. 'OK,' she said. 'Now straight to sleep. It's after midnight.'

I lay down and closed my eyes, but I wasn't able to sleep. I couldn't help thinking about Daisy. Once upon a time, she had been a young girl like me. She had secrets and hopes and dreams, like me.

I knew from the diary that Daisy had slept in this exact room.

Did she look at the crack in the ceiling over the bed, like I did every night?

Did she imagine it was a mysterious river, the way I did?

Did she look at the moon shining through the window?

Did she imagine it watching over her, protecting her?

Could she ever, ever have imagined that one

day, men would walk on the surface of the moon?

I had so many questions; they were beginning to hurt my head.

When Daisy left this place, why didn't she take her precious diary with her?

Why did she leave it hidden in a dirty old shed?

What had happened to her?

◎ ❀ ✿

Next morning, I felt kind of weird, like I'd had really vivid dreams that I couldn't shake free of. Only it wasn't dreams – it was Daisy's words that were echoing backwards and forwards through my head.

Kate and I sat in our garden for a while. I tried to concentrate on what Kate was saying, but I guess I wasn't doing a very good job. In the end, she took me by the shoulders, and shook me.

'Hello?' she said. 'Earth to Eva? Are you in there? You're not listening to a word I'm saying.'

I knew the time had come to confess.

'Sorry,' I said. 'It's just that I've been reading the diary – I'm nearly halfway through it, and I've kind of got caught up in Daisy's life. She was really—'

Kate didn't let me finish. 'You read the diary?'

I felt ashamed as she stared at me. 'It's just that it's ancient,' I said. 'Everything I read about happened years and years ago – to someone we've never even met.'

'It's still a diary!' said Kate.

Then she smiled. 'But maybe I'm a bit weird about things like that. What's she like, this Daisy person?'

'She seems like a nice girl – sort of gentle and sweet, but funny too. She loves plants and animals and stars and stuff.'

'Like me,' said Kate.

'Yeah, exactly like you – and that makes me

think that if Daisy was around now, I'd like to be friends with her.'

Kate smiled. 'So what did she do all day, back in 1947?'

'Kind of the same stuff we do. Listen to this.'

I pulled the diary from my pocket and began to read.

Dear Diary,

Today Mammy made a special picnic for Rose and me. There were cheese sandwiches and milk and a bun for each of us. We took the picnic to Manning's Field, and after we'd finished eating, we climbed the big tree, and pretended it was a magic ship. We pretended we were fancy ladies sailing away to France. It was a very happy day.

I stopped reading and gave a big sigh. 'Do you know where Manning's Field is, Kate?' I asked. 'Maybe we could go there some day, and hang out. It would be kind of cool being where

Daisy and Rose used to go, don't you think?'

At first Kate didn't answer. She was sitting there with her mouth half-open and a mysterious smile on her face.

'OMG,' she said in the end.

'What?' I asked.

'Manning's Field,' she said. 'That's the field where Jeremy is.'

'OMG, is right,' I said. 'That means Daisy and Rose used to hang out in our special place. They used to climb Jeremy too. That's totally cool.'

Kate leaned closer. 'Tell me more about Daisy,' she said.

I smiled, glad to see that at last she was really interested in the diary. I thought back to all the things I'd read the night before.

'Even though her dad was from France, Daisy was born in Seacove. She loved it here. She writes about it like it's the most magical, special place in the whole world.'

'It is,' said Kate, grinning. 'What else does she say?'

'Daisy wanted to get a scholarship to go to the secondary school in the next town,' I said. 'So she was studying a lot. She dreamed of being a children's nurse. She loved children, and hated being an only child.'

'That's sweet,' said Kate. 'That's kind of the way I felt before Simon came along.'

'Mmmm. It is sweet,' I said. 'I wish we could find out more about Daisy, though.'

'Perfect timing,' said Kate, jumping up. 'Here comes Martha. Maybe she can help us. Maybe she remembers Daisy.'

I got up too, and went over to Kate's granny who was just walking past our gate. We told her all about how we'd found the diary in the shed.

'It belongs to Daisy Lavelle,' said Kate. 'She used to live in Monica's house.'

Martha stopped walking and leaned on her stick.

'Daisy Lavelle,' she sighed. 'Now there's a name I haven't heard for fifty years or more.'

I started to get excited. 'OMG, you remember her! That's brilliant. What was she like?'

Martha shook her head. 'I'm sorry. I can't tell you much about Daisy. I never really knew her well. She was a bit older than me, and her family left here when I was very little.'

'Oh,' I said, trying to hide my disappointment.

'Where did they go?' asked Kate. 'Why did they leave?'

Martha sighed again. 'No one around here ever really trusted Daisy's father,' she said. 'Because he was French.'

'How did a French man end up living in Seacove all those years ago?' asked Kate.

'I believe he came on a visit with a rich uncle of his,' said Martha. 'And while he was here, he met Daisy's mum and they fell in love. The uncle had to go back to France on his own.'

'That's so romantic,' I sighed.

'I don't get why the local people didn't trust him,' said Kate. 'I think being French is kind of cool.'

'Things were different back in the olden days,' said Martha. 'Someone from the next parish would have been considered a bit of a threat, and someone from another country – well that was just shocking altogether. People back then didn't like the exotic – they liked when things stayed the same.'

'And is that why Daisy's family left?' I asked. 'Because they weren't really accepted around here?'

'I don't think that was the reason,' said Martha.

'Then what was?' asked Kate.

'We've read her diary,' I said. 'And we know she loved it here. So why would she leave?'

'I think there was some kind of big scandal,' said Martha. 'But I don't know any of the details.'

Kate giggled. 'It doesn't sound like a whole lot of exciting stuff happened back then,' she said. 'So how come you don't remember a big scandal?'

Martha smiled at her. 'It's hard for you young girls to understand how things used to be. In those days, children were told nothing. We weren't encouraged to ask questions. "Children should be seen and not heard" was one of my mother's favourite sayings.'

'That's just weird,' I muttered.

'Whenever my parents talked about the Lavelles,' continued Martha smiling. 'It was in whispers, and if they saw me lurking around, they would quickly start to talk about other things.'

'And didn't you ask what happened?' I said.

Martha sighed. 'Of course I asked. I asked many times. I was very fond of Daisy – she always treated me like her little pet. After they left, I sometimes went and sat in her garden, waiting for her to come back – but she never did.'

'That's so sad,' said Kate.

'In the end I stopped asking about her,' said Martha. 'Whenever I mentioned Daisy's name, my mother got very angry with me, and I didn't understand why. I was only a little girl, and after a while, I'd almost forgotten that Daisy ever existed. I never knew the truth about what happened, so I can't tell you any more, I'm afraid.'

'Oh,' I said. 'Thanks anyway, Martha.'

'You're welcome,' she said. 'It's always nice to talk about the olden days. They were such happy, innocent times.'

The olden days didn't sound all that great to me, if whole families could just vanish without the neighbouring kids knowing why or how. But I just smiled at Martha, and then she continued on her walk.

Kate and I went to the beach for a while. We

talked about all kinds of stuff, but I couldn't concentrate properly. How could I live in the present, while Daisy was always at the edge of my thoughts, distracting me?

Chapter Five

The next morning, I had more important, present-day things to worry about though. Kate called over and she didn't look happy.

'I can't stay long,' she said. 'Martha's got a last-minute appointment in the hospital for her annual check-up, and we have to leave in half an hour.'

'Why do you have to go?' I asked, not looking forward to a whole day without any of my friends around.

'Martha has to stay in hospital overnight, so while she's there, Dad's taking me on a one-night camping trip – he knows a place not far from there.'

'That sounds like a good plan,' I said. 'And you love going camping with your dad, so why do you look like it's the worst day of your life?'

'It's Zoe,' said Kate. 'She left the computer switched on last night, and I could see the website she'd been on.'

'And?'

Tears came to Kate's eyes. 'She'd been looking at a job search website – based in London. She wants to go back there, Eva. I just know it.'

I hugged her, not sure of what to say to make things better.

'And it wouldn't be just Zoe leaving,' said Kate. 'If she goes back to London, Dad and Simon would go with her too.'

'But they'd never just go off and leave you, would they? Not when you're all so happy together. These days you lot are like an ad for the perfect family.'

Kate shrugged. 'I guess Dad and Zoe would

want to take me with them,' she said.

'Then it's not a problem, is it? London's not a million miles away, and it's an amazing place to live. My friend Ruby loves it there now. I'd miss you, but I could visit you there sometimes.'

'But . . .'

'You and me and Ruby could do heaps of cool stuff together in London, and maybe you could come and stay with me here in Seacove in the summer, and—'

'Martha would never, ever go to London,' said Kate. 'She says she's never lived anywhere except for Seacove and she's too old to change that now. And if Martha won't go with Dad and Zoe, then I couldn't go either. How could I leave her here on her own? She took care of me for years when I had no one else. I couldn't just abandon her now.'

She was right. 'Maybe you could . . .' I stopped talking, because I realised I had nothing to say. I had no solution to offer my friend.

'I've got really used to Dad and Zoe and Simon being here,' she said. 'If they left now, everything would be different – and not in a good way.'

I couldn't argue with that. Martha is lovely, but I'd always thought that it was kind of lonely for Kate, living in a tiny village with just an old lady for company.

'If I can't leave, I have to find a way to make Zoe stay here, Eva,' said Kate. 'I just have to.'

'You could lock her up in the house and hide all the keys,' I said. 'Then she couldn't go anywhere.'

Kate looked all shocked, like I was being serious.

'I'm kidding!' I said. 'Anyway, it's not about stopping Zoe from leaving – it's about making her want to stay.'

'And how are we going to do that?'

'You said she was bored here – so we need to find her a job. What did she work at in London?'

'She was a personal assistant to the manager of a big hotel. She kind of did everything.'

'And are there any jobs like that in Seacove?' I asked, not feeling too optimistic about the answer.

Kate shook her head. 'There aren't any big hotels around here.'

'Maybe she could work at something else? Zoe's kind of open-minded, isn't she? I bet she'd be prepared to try pretty much anything.'

'Yeah, you're right. I think she would try anything. Only trouble is, there aren't any jobs. I've been reading the local paper and last week, the only job was for a window cleaner.'

'You think she'd like to be a window-cleaner?'

Kate made a face. 'I was desperate, so for a day or two I kind of hinted that Zoe should apply for it. I kept going on about how nice it would be to work in the open air and stuff.'

'And what happened?'

'Zoe said window-cleaning would be the

perfect job for her, except for one tiny detail.'

'Which was?'

Kate started to laugh. 'Zoe's terrified of heights.'

I laughed too, but stopped when I realised that Kate was serious again.

'You'll think of something, won't you, Eva?' she asked. 'You'll find a way to make Zoe stay?'

I nodded slowly. 'Er, sure,' I said. 'I'll think of something.'

'Brilliant,' said Kate. 'Now I've got to go help Dad to pack up the tent.'

And she ran off happily, leaving me with no idea what I was going to do next.

✿ ★ ✩

Just as I went back inside, Mum and Dad's friend, Jacob, called over. Mum and Dad greeted him like they hadn't seen him for months, which was a bit weird since they'd been in his pub only the night before. Sometimes I think Mum and Dad need to get out more.

Mum made a big pot of tea, and the three of them sat at the kitchen table talking. They talked about banks, and the weather, and the price of cabbages, until I was practically asleep from the boredom of it all.

My eyes were just closing when I caught the end of a sentence: '… no idea how I'm going to replace him,' said Jacob.

Suddenly I was wide awake. 'Replace who?' I said. 'Have you got a job that needs filling in the pub?'

Jacob laughed. 'Yes, there's a sudden vacancy, but I think you might be a little young for the job.'

'It's not for me,' I said. 'But I know someone else who's looking for a job.'

Now Jacob was really interested. 'Can they sing?' he asked.

'You need a singer?' I asked.

He nodded. 'Yes, the guy who sings in the pub

at night quit suddenly yesterday, and I urgently need a replacement.

I jumped up. 'Don't go anywhere,' I said to Jacob, and then I ran from the house and over to Kate's place. The car was just leaving and I had to practically throw myself under it to catch their attention. Patrick and Martha were arguing about the best way to get to the hospital. Kate wound down her window, rolling her eyes.

'Save me,' she whispered. 'I know Dad and Martha are going to argue for the whole journey. I'll be in need of a hospital bed by the time we get there.'

'That's not important now,' I said. 'Just tell me quickly. Can Zoe sing?'

'She sings Simon to sleep every night,' she said.

That was good enough for me. I turned to run back home. 'But Eva,' Kate called after me. I ignored her. 'You just go and have a lovely time with your dad,' I said. 'And by the time you get back, all your problems will be sorted.'

'But, Eva!' said Kate again.

Once again I ignored her as I ran inside to tell Jacob the good news.

Chapter Six

That afternoon, I walked to the pub with Zoe for her job audition. She was wheeling Simon in his buggy.

'I'm not sure this is an entirely good idea,' said Zoe.

I tried to sound all adult and sensible.

'Kate told me that you'd like to find a job,' I said.

'That's true,' said Zoe. 'I *would* like to find a job. Much as I love my little boy, being at home with him all day isn't enough for me.'

'So a part time job is exactly what you want. You'll meet loads of new people if you work in a bar. And you love singing,' I said. 'So this is perfect for you.'

She still wasn't convinced. 'I do like singing,' she said. 'And I know Simon loves my voice, but I'm not sure if I'm quite good enough for the pub. I've never really sung in public before.'

'It'll be fine,' I said. 'Jacob said that Declan, the guitar player, is brilliant. He'll help you out if you're nervous. You'll be great, just wait and see.'

So – because Zoe is a really happy, optimistic person – she smiled at me, and walked a bit faster, with a kind of excited spring in her step.

And I walked a bit behind her, with my fingers crossed, hoping things were going to turn out as I had planned.

☆ ♥ ♡

Twenty minutes later, I was sitting in a corner of the bar, with Simon on my knee. Zoe was standing on a small platform near the window, holding a microphone. Next to her sat Declan, a smiley-faced man who was tuning a guitar. Jacob was standing behind the bar counter, polishing glasses. The only customers were two old ladies who were drinking coffee and chatting.

'All in your own time,' said Declan to Zoe. 'Just tell me when you're ready.'

Zoe looked really, really nervous. I gave her a big thumbs-up sign, and Simon clapped his hands enthusiastically, almost like he knew what was going on.

Zoe smiled. 'OK,' she said in a shaky voice. 'It's now or never.'

Declan began to strum his guitar, and a few seconds later, Zoe started to sing. Well, actually, she opened her mouth and noises came out, but it wasn't like any singing I'd ever heard in my life before. Her voice was screechy, like fingernails on a blackboard. Jacob stopped polishing glasses, and stood there with his mouth wide open. One of the old ladies took out her hearing aid and adjusted it. The other old lady was looking frantically at the door, like she was planning to escape. Simon closed his eyes and laid his head on my shoulder. I thought that was a strange response, but I was too busy figuring out what was going on to worry about it.

Declan continued to play, but he had a weird look on his face, like he was going to faint or die or something. As the song continued, Zoe kept randomly speeding up and slowing down, and I could see that Declan was struggling in a big way.

I sat there, not knowing if I should laugh or cry.

Finally, after what felt like about ten years, the song came to an end. Zoe put down the microphone and smiled at everyone.

'That went better than I'd expected,' she said, though I'm not sure anyone except me was still listening.

Jacob came over and shook her hand. 'Well done, Zoe,' he said.

'So is the job mine?' she asked.

The poor man looked totally embarrassed. 'Your voice is lovely and everything, but I'm not sure your style of singing is exactly what I'm looking for. I'm sorry.'

'Oh,' said Zoe, with a hurt look. Then she took Simon from my arms and went outside to strap him into his buggy.

As I followed her, I heard Declan talking to Jacob. 'I don't want to be mean or anything,' he said. 'But if you hire her, I'm leaving. I've never …'

I closed the door, so I wouldn't have to listen any more, and Zoe and I set off for home.

'I was rubbish, wasn't I?' she said.

'I'm not sure "rubbish" is the word I'd use.'

This was the truth. 'Rubbish' didn't begin to describe the awful sounds she'd made. I wished I'd been brave enough to protect my ears. I was beginning to worry that I'd damaged my hearing forever.

'Jacob didn't like my singing,' she said. 'I could see it in his eyes. But hey, it's no big deal. You can't be good at everything, right?'

'Right,' I said.

Zoe put one arm around me. 'It was nice of you to try to get me a job, Eva,' she said. 'And since you're such a kind girl, can you do me one more favour?'

'Sure,' I said. 'What do you want?'

'Could you promise never to tell Kate or Patrick about this afternoon? If they hear what happened, I will never, ever be allowed to forget it.'

I'd encouraged the poor woman to make an idiot of herself in public, so the least I could do was make that small promise.

'Forget what?' I said, and the two of us laughed the rest of the way home.

I met Kate for a few minutes when she got back

the next day.

'Dad and I had an amazing time,' she said. 'It was just like the camping trips we used to have years ago, before he went to live in London.'

'I'm glad,' I said. 'I know Zoe is great, but it's probably good for you and your dad to have time together too.'

'Oh yeah – speaking of Zoe. You asked me yesterday if she could sing, but you ran off before I could finish answering you.'

'Did I?' I asked, trying not to look guilty. 'What were you going to say?'

'I was going to say that she's a really bad singer.'

'But you said that she sings Simon to sleep every night.'

Kate laughed. 'She does – and within seconds of her opening her mouth, Simon closes his eyes. Dad and I joke about it when Zoe's not listening. We think Simon just pretends to be asleep, so Zoe will be quiet.'

I remembered what Simon had done the day before. The poor little kid had been pretending to be asleep!

'Zoe's so bad it's almost funny,' continued Kate. 'But why were you asking about her and singing?'

'Oh, you know,' I said as vaguely as I could. 'I was just wondering.'

♡ ♔ ♚

That night, I saw Daisy's diary on the table next to my bed.

'I'm sorry, Daisy,' I whispered. 'I almost forgot about you, I was so busy trying to fix up a job for Zoe.'

I don't usually talk to diaries, but I couldn't help it. In a weird way, I felt like Daisy was my friend, like she was talking to me, like she wanted me to know her story.

As I picked up the diary, something fell out and slid across the floor. I had to jump out of bed and almost crawl under the wardrobe to find it. It was an ancient old black and white photograph of a man and a woman, and a girl with a big floppy ribbon in her curly hair. The girl was pretty, with huge dark, laughing eyes. All three were holding hands. They looked happy.

I turned the photograph over. There was writing on the back –

Jean-Marc, Florrie and Daisy Lavelle. April 1947

'Daisy,' I sighed. 'Whatever happened to you? Where did you go to? And why?'

I looked at the photograph for a long time, and then I picked up the diary and settled down to read.

'Eva! It's the middle of the night. Why is your light still on?'

It was dad, and he was cross – until he looked at me properly. Then he ran over to my bed.

'What is it, my darling?' he asked. 'Why are you crying?'

He handed me a tissue, but it wasn't enough for the streams of tears that were rolling down my face. Dad hugged me for a long time, and didn't seem to mind that his favourite t-shirt was getting all gross and soggy.

'Tell me, Eva,' he said, when I'd recovered a bit. 'Tell me what's happened.'

So I wiped my eyes on my sheet, took a deep breath and told him what I'd discovered.

Telling Daisy's story felt kind of strange, since it had all happened so many years ago, but once I started, I couldn't stop. When I was finished, Dad hugged me again.

'That's a really sad story, Eva,' he said. 'But for all you know, things might have been fine in the end. Try not to worry about the poor girl.'

'OK, Dad. I'll try that,' I said as he pulled the covers over me and I snuggled down to sleep.

Then I spent the rest of the night lying awake and worrying about Daisy.

Chapter Seven

♫

When I called over to Kate's place the next morning, it was so early that she was still in bed. While her dad went up to get her, I chatted to Zoe, and played with Simon, who luckily didn't seem to have any lasting bad effects from Zoe's disastrous singing exploits.

When Kate came downstairs, she was dressed, but her hair was all messy and she was rubbing her eyes.

'This had better be important, Eva,' she said. 'I need all the beauty sleep I can get.'

'It *is* important,' I said. 'Really important. Now, do you want to go to Jeremy, and I'll tell you all about it?'

We were headed for the door, when Kate's dad called her back. 'You're not going anywhere without breakfast, young lady,' he said. 'Breakfast is the most important meal of the day.'

Kate rolled her eyes, grabbed a banana from the fruit bowl, and then we ran from the room before her dad had time to protest.

'I'm guessing this has something to do with Daisy?' said Kate, as we got to our favourite place on the grass near the trunk of the huge tree.

'Yes,' I said, as I pulled the diary from my jacket pocket. 'It's about Daisy. Now make yourself comfortable while I tell you the saddest story in the whole wide world.'

Kate rested her back against the tree, and stretched her legs out in front of her.

'I'm ready,' she said. 'So start talking.'

'As you know, in the beginning, Daisy's life was kind of boring,' I began. 'A day of collecting blackberries was like an amazing event, and finding a new kind of seaweed was the most exciting thing ever. Mostly she just went to school, and hung out with her friend Rose, and helped her mum and dad around the house.'

'That sounds a bit like my life,' said Kate.

I grinned. 'Maybe. Except without TV and a computer and a phone and useful stuff like that. Anyway, all of a sudden, things changed. Daisy's life got a whole lot more exciting – and not in a good way.'

'What happened?' Kate asked, edging closer to me.

'I'll let Daisy explain in her own words,' I said, as I carefully flicked through the pages until I found the one I wanted.

Kate lay back on the grass and I began to read.

Dear Diary,

Today something very strange happened. Garda Dillon came to the house and Daddy asked him in for a cup of tea and a slice of fruitcake that Mammy had just taken out of the oven. Garda Dillon went all red in the face and said it wasn't a social call. He asked could Daddy go to the garda station with him to talk about a crime. Mammy cried all the time that Daddy was gone, and I didn't know what to do to make her stop. When Daddy came back he hugged us both and said it was all a misunderstanding and we should forget about it. We had tea then; the fruitcake was lovely.

'That doesn't sound too serious,' said Kate when I stopped reading.

'That's what I thought – and that's probably what Daisy thought too, but unfortunately we were all wrong.'

'So did you find out what the crime was?'

'Yes. Somebody broke into a church in

Newtown and stole a chalice.'

'And was that such a big deal? It's not like he held up a bank or something!'

'The chalice was really old and really valuable, but that wasn't the only reason it was a big deal. People were very religious back then, and stealing a chalice was like a super-big crime. The teachers in Daisy's school got the kids to say prayers every morning, so that the chalice would be found and the thief sent to jail.'

'But surely Daisy's dad wasn't involved?'

'That's what I thought too, and at first things went on pretty much as before. Then, a few weeks later, Daisy's dad was charged with the crime, and he had to go to court. This is what she wrote:

Dear Diary,

Daddy's court case is tomorrow. Mammy spent a long time ironing his clothes, so he would look decent for the judge. She was crying so much, though, tears kept falling on his good white shirt and ruining it. In the end, I had to do it for her. Daddy says Mammy is upsetting herself over nothing. He said, 'I haven't done anything wrong, so I don't have to be afraid. I will just tell the truth, and that will be the end of that. Justice is always done in the end.' Daddy would never tell a lie, so I know it will all work out well.

Now Kate sat up. 'You said it was a sad story, so I'm guessing things didn't turn out the way Daisy hoped.'

I shook my head. 'The trial only lasted for one day.'

'And?'

'And Daisy's dad was found guilty and sentenced to five years in jail.'

'Ouch!' said Kate. 'That's awful. So what happened to Daisy?'

'Some of the next entries are kind of rushed and untidy – like she was too upset to concentrate properly. Whole days go by and she doesn't write anything at all. The kids in her class gave her a hard time because her dad was in prison.'

'And didn't the teachers step in?'

'It doesn't sound like it. Remember they were the ones who were organising prayer meetings for the safe return of the chalice. I'm guessing they gave Daisy a hard time too. Soon she stopped going to school altogether.'

'But what about her scholarship?'

'The scholarship was the least of her worries,' I said. 'Listen to what she wrote a month after her dad went to jail:

Dear Diary,

The good china is getting dusty, because it is never used – Mammy's friends don't come to see her any more. When Mammy and I went to Mass last week, everyone pointed at us and whispered.

Rose waved at me from the other side of the church. She

started to come over to us, but her mammy pulled her back.

Mammy cries all the time now. I try to cheer her up but nothing works. She used to be so proud of her glossy hair and her trim figure, but now she doesn't care about anything. She sits at the kitchen table and drinks tea and eats so much bread that she is getting fat. Some days she doesn't get up out of bed at all. I don't know what is going to happen to her. I don't know what is going to happen to me.

'OMG,' said Kate. 'The poor girl. She didn't do anything to deserve this. None of it is her fault, and yet her whole world is collapsing around her. People must have been really mean back then.'

'I know,' I said, wondering if people would act differently nowadays. 'It's totally unfair.'

'So how did Daisy survive like that until her dad got back?'

I sighed. 'I'm not finished yet. I'm afraid

things got even worse. Daisy's mum couldn't cope at all. In the end, she was so bad that she had to go to some kind of a psychiatric hospital.'

'And did they make her better?'

I shook my head. 'No. I don't think psychiatric hospitals made people better back in the olden days. It sounds like they locked poor Florrie up and threw away the key.'

'And Daisy?'

'In a way, she was lucky. She had a great aunt who lived in America, and arrangements were made to send Daisy to live with her.'

'And she left her diary behind?'

'Yes, but not by accident. This is her last entry:

Dear Diary,

Yesterday I went to see Mammy in the hospital and Daddy in the prison. We all cried for a long time. Mammy and Daddy both told me to be brave, but that is not easy. I am leaving for the boat first thing in the morning. I am afraid of travelling alone. I have never been anywhere without Mammy and Daddy before. Rose gave me her bracelet to bring me luck. I will miss her very much. I am not going to bring this diary to America. I am going to hide it in my secret place at the back of the old hen-house. When Daddy's name is cleared, things will be different. I will come back home to Seacove and Mammy will come out of hospital. We will have visitors and people will be nice to us again. I will go back to school and study for my scholarship. I will fill all the rest of these pages with happy stories.

Goodbye for a while, my dear diary.

I stopped reading and wiped the tears from my eyes. It might have been kind of embarrassing, except that Kate was crying too. We hugged for a bit, and then we sat back on the grass. It was weird, crying about something that had happened so long ago, to someone we had never met. It was almost like crying at a movie.

'The poor girl never came back?' said Kate in

the end.

'That's what it looks like. This diary was really important to her, but she never wrote in it again.'

'So I'm guessing it's been lying in the shed, untouched, since 1947,' she said. 'It's like it was waiting for her.'

'No,' I said, feeling suddenly excited. 'Maybe the diary wasn't waiting for Daisy. Maybe it was waiting for us!'

Much later we were still discussing it.

'It's obvious,' I said for the tenth time. 'Daisy said she wouldn't come back until her dad's name was cleared. She never touched her diary again, so that must never have happened.'

'It's not obvious at all,' said Kate, who loves a good argument. 'Maybe Daisy's dad *was* cleared. Maybe he was released from prison, and her mum got better and they went off to America to live with Daisy, and the three of them lived happily ever after.'

I shook my head. 'I wish I could believe that, but I can't. It's been years and years and years. Daisy loved Seacove as much as you and I do. If her dad's name had been cleared, I *know* she would have come back at some stage. She'd have found a way to come home.'

'But—'

I didn't let her finish. 'Can't you see, Kate? When I read that diary, I felt like Daisy was talking to me. I felt like she was sending me a message from the past.'

'And her message is?' asked Kate, looking at me like I was an idiot.

Now I felt embarrassed. 'I know it sounds totally weird,' I said. 'But I can't help that. I just think that we should try to discover what really happened. I think we should find out more about the crime.'

'The Case of the Stolen Chalice,' said Kate,

giggling. 'Sounds like a *Famous Five* book.'

I ignored her. 'I wonder if we could find a way to prove that Daisy's dad was innocent. Then we should track Daisy down and let her know – if she's still alive, that is.'

Kate didn't look convinced. 'There are two kind of big 'ifs' in that sentence, you know, Eva,' she said.

'I know,' I said. 'But shouldn't we try anyway, for Daisy's sake?'

Now Kate was serious. She reached over and took my hand. 'Eva, there's one important thing you're not considering, isn't there?'

'What?'

She spoke slowly and carefully, like she was afraid of offending me.

'Maybe Daisy's dad really was guilty. Maybe he *did* break into that church. Maybe he *did* steal the chalice. Maybe justice *was* done – only not in the way Daisy was hoping.'

I shook my head. 'No way,' I said. 'Daisy's

dad would never have done a thing like that.'

'And you know that how?'

'Because Daisy said he was innocent.'

'She would say that, wouldn't she?' Kate squeezed my hand tightly. 'He was her dad,' she whispered. 'She loved him. She wanted to believe the best of him – but that doesn't necessarily mean that he was innocent.'

I didn't like what she was saying. 'But—' I began, before she interrupted me. 'Even axe-murderers probably hug their kids at night, and tell them bedtime stories. I bet lifelong criminals have kids who believe they've never done a single bad thing in their lives. Love makes people do funny things.'

'So now you're an expert on love?' I said crossly.

'Actually I am,' she said. 'When my dad left, I was really, really angry, but I never stopped loving him, not even for one second. Abandoning me was a bad thing to do, and it messed up my life for years, but when Dad came back, I forgave him. That's what love does to a person.'

I gave her a quick hug. 'I'm really glad your dad came back,' I said. 'But this is different, isn't it?'

She shook her head. 'Not really. Maybe Daisy's dad really was a bad person, but because she loved him, she couldn't face up to it. She couldn't deal with the truth.'

I sighed. 'What you say makes sense,' I said. 'But let's not give up so quickly. How about we do a bit of research and see what we come up with?'

'You're going to do this whether I agree or not aren't you?' she asked.

'Yes,' I said, already planning my next move.

She jumped up. 'OK,' she said. 'Count me in. Time for the Kate and Eva Cold-Case Detective Agency to set up for business.'

Chapter Eight

Even though she's really nice, I can never manage to forget how much Kate's granny, Martha, scared me when I met her first. Because of this, when we got to Kate's place, I was really glad to see that Martha was in a good mood.

'We need to ask you something,' I said.

'About Daisy Lavelle,' finished Kate.

'I'd dearly like to help you two girls,' said Martha. 'But I told you already – I barely remember that girl and her family. What I remember most is the bad feeling they inspired after they left. For years afterwards, people spoke about them with a sense of horror, almost as if all three of them had been evil.'

'That's totally mean,' said Kate.

Martha sighed. 'I agree with you,' she said. 'But those were different times, harder times. The war hadn't been over for long, remember.'

'Is that the Second World War?' I asked. 'We read about that in school. But I thought Ireland wasn't involved.'

Martha laughed. 'That's the trouble with history books,' she said. 'They only tell you half of the truth. Ireland might not have been directly involved, but if your nearest neighbour is at war, you can be sure that's going to have a big effect on you. Many Irish people went away to fight and there were great hardships here too, you know. People became even more suspicious and intolerant than before.'

'Sorry,' I said, feeling stupid.

'Anyway,' said Kate, changing the subject. 'Let's get back to Daisy. Can you think of anyone else who might have known her, Martha? Did she have any cousins or aunties or uncles around here or anything?'

Martha shook her head. 'As far as I know, Daisy Lavelle didn't have any family besides her mum and dad. After they left Seacove, the cottage was empty for years and years. It always struck me as a sad place. I was glad when it was finally sold when I was a teenager.'

'What about friends?' I asked. 'Daisy writes a lot about a girl called Rose.'

Now Martha smiled. 'That would have to be Rose Madigan from the Coast Road. She was a lovely girl.'

'And is she ...?' began Kate.

'Oh, she's alive and well,' said Martha. 'She lives in the nursing home on the hill overlooking the bay.'

'OMG,' I said. 'Do you think she might talk to us?'

Martha didn't answer. She suddenly got up and walked towards the kitchen.

'What's going on?' I whispered to Kate. 'Did

I say something wrong?'

'I'm not deaf, young lady,' called Martha from the kitchen. 'And nothing is wrong. I'm just doing a bit of baking. If you bring Rose a box of my famous chocolate buns she'll welcome you with open arms and tell you anything at all you need to know.'

An hour later, Kate and I were waiting in a little sitting room in the nursing home. On Kate's knees was a tin of still-warm chocolate buns. In the pocket of my hoodie I had Daisy's diary and the Lavelle family photo that Zoe had copied on her computer.

I couldn't help feeling nervous.

'You're sure Martha rang and told Rose about us?' I said.

'Yes, I'm sure. She told her that we found the photograph and the diary. She told her we want to talk about Daisy, and Rose is fine with that.

Now stop worrying, Eva. Martha said that Rose gets tired easily, so we need to concentrate, and not waste time.'

Just then the door opened and a nurse wheeled an old lady into the room. 'These are the two girls who have come to see you, Mrs Madigan,' he said.

The old lady in the wheelchair smiled at us with a sweet, wrinkled old face. She leaned over and took both of our hands tightly in her skinny ones. It was like being held by a scraggly old chicken, but I didn't like to pull away. The nurse put the brake on the wheelchair and walked towards the door.

'I'll be back in fifteen minutes, but ring the bell if you want me before that,' he said.

When he was gone, we all looked at each other for a minute. Then I pulled the photo from my pocket and held it towards Rose. She let go of our hands, took the photo and looked at it for a long time. I was beginning to wonder if she'd fallen asleep or died or something when I noticed tears streaming down her face. I scrabbled in my pockets until I found a clean(ish) tissue and handed it to Rose.

'We're so sorry,' said Kate.

'We didn't mean to upset you,' I said.

Rose wiped her eyes and gave us a watery smile. 'That's all right, girls. A little cry now and then does no harm to anyone. It was just a bit strange, seeing those dear faces again after such a long time.'

'What happened?' I asked. 'What happened to Daisy and her mum and dad in the end?'

Rose's smile faded. 'It was a terrible, terrible sad business,' she said.

I thought she was going to cry again, and I looked desperately at Kate.

Was this whole thing a really bad idea?

Were we upsetting this poor old lady for nothing?

'We know some stuff,' said Kate gently. 'We

know about the court case. We know that Daisy's dad went to jail.'

Then I couldn't resist any more.

'Did he really do it? Did Daisy's dad really steal that chalice?'

It was a long time before Rose answered. 'Mr Lavelle was a lovely man. He was handsome and good and kind. Daisy always protested his innocence, and I believed her, but in later years ....'

'In later years what?' I prompted her.

'In later years I wasn't so sure any more. Daisy and I were only children when it all happened. We were mostly kept in the dark. Mr Lavelle was convicted, so I suppose there must have been evidence against him.' She gave a big, quivery sigh. 'I'm simply not sure any more. I'm not sure of anything any more.'

For a minute no one said anything, and it was totally embarrassing. Then Rose gave a small smile.

'Daisy was the best friend I ever had,' she said. 'She was a sweet girl. After her daddy was sent to jail my parents told me I couldn't see her any more.'

'But that's so unfair,' I said. 'You and Daisy hadn't done anything wrong.'

'Daisy and I thought it was unfair too,' said Rose. 'That's why I ignored my parents' instructions.'

'What did you do?' asked Kate.

Rose smiled a dreamy smile. 'Late at night, Daisy used to sneak out of her house and come over to my place. When I heard her special whistle outside, I crept from my bed, and out the back door. We went for long moonlit walks together. We spent many hours together like this.'

Kate and I grinned at each other. That's exactly what we had done the year before.

'They were sad times,' said Rose. 'But they were special too. It felt like it was just Daisy and me against the rest of the world. But before long, things changed again …'

'We know that Daisy went to America in 1947,' said Kate. 'But what happened after that? Did she ever come back here? Did her mum get better? Did her dad get out of jail?'

'Poor Mrs Lavelle was not a strong woman,' said Rose. 'When her husband was sent to jail, she fell to pieces. She ended up in the mental home – not a very nice place to be in those days I'm afraid.'

'And how long did she have to stay there?' I asked.

'After Daisy left for America, my mother visited Mrs Lavelle a few times,' said Rose. 'But then one day she was told that Mrs Lavelle had been transferred to a locked ward, and wasn't allowed visitors.'

'But that's totally cruel,' I said. 'The poor woman.'

'A year later,' continued Rose, 'word came

that Mrs Lavelle had died. Two years after that, Mr Lavelle died in prison.'

'OMG,' I whispered. 'That's awful. Poor Daisy.'

'But what exactly happened to Mr and Mrs Lavelle?' asked Kate. 'How did they both just die?'

Rose sighed. 'Who knows? Maybe after all that had happened, they simply lost the will to live. I'm sorry I can't tell you more. You see, no one ever talked openly about the Lavelles. It was almost as if they were a guilty secret we weren't allowed to think about. It was almost as if they were a bad dream that was best forgotten.'

'And Daisy?' I asked.

'She was a dear girl and I missed her terribly,' said Rose. 'In those days, America might as well have been on another planet.'

For a second I could see past the wrinkled old lady, to the sad young girl Rose had once been.

What must have it been like for her to have

her friend leave so suddenly like that?

How awful must it have been not to be able to talk about her?

'Daisy and I wrote to each other at first,' said Rose. 'She told me all about her new life in America. It seemed exciting – but always tinged with sadness. I could tell that she was very lonely. Her great-aunt meant well, but she didn't understand young girls. She thought that Daisy should just move on and forget all about her old life.'

'She was expected to act like none of it ever happened?' said Kate angrily. 'She was expected to forget her mum, and her dad, and you and Seacove? How could she possibly do that?'

Rose sighed. 'It sounds harsh, I know. Anyway, after her daddy died, Daisy stopped writing. I waited and waited, but there was no word from her. My letters came back to me unopened. I don't know what happened to my friend, or where she went.'

I could feel tears coming to my eyes, but they embarrassed me. I'd never met Daisy or her mum and dad. Why did I care so much about what had happened to them?

Then I saw that Kate's eyes were damp too, and that made me feel a small bit better.

While I was struggling to think of something to say, the nurse came back into the room.

'All happy here?' he said brightly, not seeming to notice that the three of us were holding soggy tissues and had blotchy faces and red eyes.

'Never better,' I said, trying to smile.

Then I remembered the diary. I took it from my pocket.

'Daisy's diary,' said Rose, recognising it immediately. She stroked the leather cover with shaky fingers. 'That diary was so precious to her.'

I held it towards her. I really didn't want to part with it, but Rose had more right to it than I did.

'If you like you can ...' I began, but Rose cut me off.

'No thank you, dear' she said. 'I don't need Daisy's diary. Memories are enough for me.'

I felt relieved as I put the diary back in my pocket.

Then Kate remembered the tin on her knee.

'Chocolate buns,' she said. 'Martha made them specially for you.'

'Martha's famous chocolate buns,' said Rose. 'One of life's little pleasures.'

When we left, Rose was eating a chocolate bun, and gazing at the photo of her old friend. She was smiling, and that made me feel a small bit better. This was turning out to be a very sad story, and I was glad that giving Rose the photo of her old friend had helped a bit.

Neither Kate nor I spoke a word all the way home.

Chapter Nine

Next morning I called over for Kate. 'Come inside,' she said. 'Zoe's making a cake.'

'What's the occasion?' I asked.

'There isn't one. Zoe just likes making cakes.'

She looked around her and then whispered. 'Zoe makes the most amazing cakes ever, but I can't let Martha hear me saying that. She might be jealous.'

'But Martha makes great cakes too. Her chocolate buns are almost famous.'

'I know,' whispered Kate. 'Martha's cakes are delicious, but Zoe's are a step beyond that. They're totally delicious, and they *look* amazing too. Zoe's cakes look like they belong in a really fancy bakery in Paris or somewhere.'

By then we were in the kitchen. Zoe poured us each a big glass of home-made lemonade and then went back to decorating her cake. She rolled out some pale green icing and then used a cutter to make heaps of tiny green leaf shapes. She used little dabs of icing to stick these onto the top of a perfectly smooth round cake.

'That is totally amazing, Zoe,' I said. 'Kate's right, you're a genius cake-maker.'

'Thanks,' said Zoe. 'But enough about cakes, already. Kate told me what happened yesterday. I think that has to be the saddest story I've ever heard.'

'It's definitely the saddest story I've ever heard,' I said. 'I couldn't sleep last night, thinking about poor Daisy. How could so many bad things happen to one person? It just doesn't seem fair.'

'So what are you going to do about it?' asked Zoe.

'Do?' I asked. 'What can we do? We can't change the fact that Daisy's dad went to jail, or the fact that her mother was sent to hospital just because she was sad. We can't change the fact that both her parents died. And anyway, maybe none of it matters. For all we know, Daisy could be dead by now too.'

'Put that stuff aside for a moment,' said Zoe. 'Do you believe that Daisy's dad was innocent?'

'Kate asked me the exact same thing yesterday,' I said. 'Are you two part of a big anti-Mr Lavelle conspiracy?'

Kate and Zoe grinned at each other. 'We just want to know the truth,' said Kate.

'The truth is always good,' said Zoe, giving her a big, soppy smile.

It was totally cute seeing Kate and Zoe get on so well, but I just rolled my eyes and pretended to be grossed-out.

'Anyway,' I said. 'I've been thinking about that very question, and I remembered something I read the other day.'

I pulled Daisy's diary from my pocket. I flicked through the pages until I found the one I wanted.

'Daisy wrote this months before the whole affair of the chalice happened,' I said, as I began to read aloud.

Dear Diary,

Daddy was late for supper tonight. He'd gone to the market to buy feed for the chickens and on the way home he realized that Jack Murphy had given him sixpence too much in his change. So he cycled two miles to Murphy's farm to give it back. Daddy was drenched wet when he got home. He only laughed when Mammy made a fuss, and said he'd catch a deathly cold. 'Honesty will keep me warm,' he said, and even Mammy had to laugh then.

I closed the diary. 'Does that sound like a man who would steal anything?' I asked.

Zoe and Kate shook their heads. 'Definitely

not,' they said together.

'But it was all so long ago,' said Kate. 'Even if Mr Lavelle was wrongly convicted, what can we do about it now?'

'It's never too late to make a wrong right,' said Zoe.

'Cool saying,' I said. 'Did you just make that up?'

Zoe laughed. 'Not exactly. My Grandma embroidered it on a sampler and hung it on her kitchen wall. She quoted it to me about five times every day.'

Kate jumped up. 'Come on, Eva,' she said. 'What are you waiting for? We've got a wrong to right – and I think I know exactly where to start.'

Gerry the friendly policeman remembered us from when we'd saved Jeremy from being destroyed. He brought us into the waiting room of the police station, and told us to sit down.

'Hello, girls,' he said when we were all settled. 'What brings you here? Are you trying to save more trees? That was mighty work you did against that developer guy.'

Kate giggled. 'No,' she said. 'We're not here about a tree this time. It's something different altogether.'

'So tell me more,' said Gerry.

'We need to talk to you about a crime,' I said. 'It happened very near here – in Newtown.'

Gerry reached for a notebook, and fluttered through the pages until he found a blank one. Then he took a pencil from the top pocket of his uniform.

'Take your time and give me all the details,' he said. 'What was the nature of the crime?'

'A very valuable silver chalice was stolen,' said Kate.

Gerry wrote something down. 'And when exactly did this happen?'

'In 1947,' I said. 'In September.'

Gerry put down the pencil and looked at us over his glasses.

'Is this some kind of joke you girls are playing?' he asked. 'I presume you know that wasting police time is a crime.'

I rushed to explain. 'We know it was ages and ages ago, but we think the wrong person was blamed.'

'And that man went to jail, and his family broke up,' said Kate.

Gerry put away his notebook and pencil, and sat back on his chair. He listened patiently while Kate and I told the sad story of the Lavelle family.

When we were finished, Gerry shook his head. 'That's tragic,' he said. 'A tragic affair altogether. But I'm afraid I don't understand why you're telling me. All that happened many years ago, long before I was even born.'

'We thought maybe you'd have the files here

in the police station,' I said. 'Maybe you could show them to us. Maybe Kate and I could look at the evidence. Maybe we could ......'

I stopped talking when I realised that what I was saying sounded kind of stupid. This wasn't a glitzy American TV detective show. Kate and I weren't going to be able to access shiny labs with microscopes and fancy computer programmes that could check for ancient fingerprints. We were just kids and we were way, way out of our depth.

Gerry was kind enough not to laugh.

'I'm sorry, girls,' he said. 'We don't have much storage space here. Files from 1947 would have been sent to Head Office many years ago. And even if I had the files here with me, I couldn't just hand them out to anyone who showed up here with a sad story. There are confidentiality issues here, and I have to follow the rules.'

'We understand,' I said, as Kate and I stood up. 'We shouldn't have bothered you.'

I felt small and stupid as Gerry shook our hands and showed us to the door.

'That was a rubbish idea of mine,' said Kate as soon as the policeman had gone back inside.

I shrugged. 'It seemed OK at the time,' I said. 'And it's not like I had any better ideas anyway.'

'So now what?'

'Maybe we should face up to the fact that there's nothing we can do. Maybe Daisy's story ends right here.'

Just then the door of the police station opened again.

'I've had an idea that might help you,' said Gerry. 'The big library in town keeps copies of all the local newspapers. Back in the forties they used to have very comprehensive court reports. Maybe you could find something to help you there.'

I felt like hugging him, but figured there was probably a law against it!

So Kate and I just thanked him and then

we raced off to get our bikes for the cycle in to town.

☼ ☾ ✿

The woman in the library was really nice and helpful. She told Kate and me to sit at a big wide table, and before long she was back with a stack of dusty old newspapers.

'Here you go,' she said, putting them on the table in front of us. 'Everything you need should be here.'

'Thanks so much,' I said.

The librarian smiled. 'The fact that you knew exactly which dates you wanted made my job very easy. Court reports are usually on the second last page. Now, I'll leave you to it. Just give me a call if you need anything else.'

It didn't take us long to find the report of Daisy's father's court case. Seeing it in black and white newsprint made it seem even more real than before. I thought of all the people in

Seacove reading it, and believing it, and slowly beginning to hate Mr Lavelle and his family.

Kate and I leaned closer to the page, to read the small fuzzy text. The report was short, and to the point.

'OMG,' whispered Kate when we'd both finished reading. 'There was a witness to the crime! This George Eades person says he saw Jean-Marc Lavelle leaving the church in Newtown with the chalice under his arm!'

'I don't believe that. George Eades had to be lying.'

Kate looked at the report again. 'That's what Jean-Marc said in court. Jean-Marc said he wasn't anywhere near the church at the time.'

'That's just weird. If two people stand up in court, and say completely opposite things, why would everyone believe one and not the other?'

'Remember what Martha said about people back then being suspicious of foreigners? Remember the war was just over, and people were kind of mixed up. Maybe it was too easy for them to believe that the foreigner, the man from France, had to be the liar.'

'So everyone automatically trusted the local guy?'

Kate nodded. 'I guess so.'

'But that's so unfair!'

Kate nodded again. 'I agree.'

For a minute I felt really, really angry. How cruel was it for everyone to judge Jean-Marc because of the way he looked and the way he spoke? Didn't anyone ever stop to consider his feelings?

But then Kate looked up at me, and I remembered what she was like when I first met her. Back then I decided I didn't like her just because she had messy hair and didn't wear cool clothes.

'What?' she asked.

I realised I was staring at her. 'Oh, nothing,' I said quickly. 'I was just thinking that sometimes people can't help being prejudiced. What's important now is that we try to make things right again.'

'But how?'

'Er, I'm not sure yet. Just give me a bit of time, and I'll think of something.'

We tidied up the newspapers and took them back to the desk.

'You girls don't look very happy,' the librarian said. 'Weren't you able to find what you were looking for?'

'Yes and no,' I said. 'We found something, but it's not what we'd hoped for.'

'Thanks anyway,' said Kate, and then the two of us went back to her place to try to come up with a plan.

Chapter Ten

Patrick was playing with Simon in the garden when we got back. We told him about our failed morning at the police station and the library.

'So now what are you going to do?' he asked.

Kate and I shrugged. 'We're all out of ideas,' I said.

'I know,' said Patrick. 'Why don't you study the stars? The answer is always in the stars.'

''tars,' said Simon, pointing up at the sky.

'That's a totally brilliant idea, Dad,' said Kate. 'We can draw up charts and stuff, and plan what to do next.'

'And there's a full moon tonight,' said Patrick.

'Conditions should be just perfect for prophecies and predictions.'

I watched as the two of them went on about the stars. Kate and her dad argue a lot, so I was totally glad to see them agreeing about something. Only thing was, I wished they weren't agreeing on something so totally weird.

How were the stars supposed to tell us what to do?

Then I noticed that Kate and Patrick were rolling on the grass, laughing.

'Your face was so funny,' said Kate. 'You looked like you wanted to choke or something.'

'I knew you were kidding,' I lied.

'Sorry, Eva,' said Patrick. 'I couldn't resist teasing you.'

Kate was wiping her eyes. 'Everyone confuses astrology and astronomy, Eva,' she said.

'They do?'

'Dad's hobby is astronomy,' she said patiently. 'That's basically looking at stars and stuff and studying them. Astrology is totally different. Astrologers believe that stars can influence your personality and change your life. Dad and I think that's kind of weird.'

Kate must have guessed how embarrassed I felt. 'It's OK,' she said. 'It was totally mean of Dad to tease you like that.'

Patrick stood up. 'Kate, do you think you could watch Simon for a bit? I've got some work to do – and the stars predict that this is a good time for me to do it.'

Then, after he and Kate had had another good laugh, he went inside.

Kate lay on the grass and Simon sat on top of her belly. For the next twenty minutes, he bounced up and down, while tickling her nose with a long stalk of grass. This made them both laugh like maniacs.

It was funny watching them, and even funnier when Kate pushed Simon's bottom off her face.

'Eeew, Simon, that's gross,' she screeched.

'Dad! Zoe! Come quickly!'

Zoe came running out, looking worried.

'What's wrong?' she asked. 'Is someone hurt?'

'Worse than that,' said Kate. 'There's a nappy emergency.'

Zoe picked Simon up and hugged him. (I'm not sure how she could bring herself to do that as the smell had already reached me, and it was totally disgusting. Maybe mums get special hormones so they don't notice stuff like that.)

'Is your big sister bullying you again, Simon?' Zoe asked. 'She's a very naughty big sister, isn't she?'

Kate made a face at me, but I knew she was pleased. She totally loves being a big sister – even to a baby who was wearing the stinkiest nappy I'd ever smelled.

Zoe took Simon inside to change his nappy, and when she came out again, she sat on the grass beside us.

'I've been dying to tell you two the great

news,' she said. 'While Simon was having his nap this morning, I did some more research on the internet. I managed to trace Daisy's arrival in New York. She got there on the 15th of November 1947.'

'That's amazing,' I said. 'Then what happened?'

Zoe gave a big sigh. 'That's it, I'm afraid. I couldn't get any further. After Daisy's arrival in New York, it's as if she vanished into thin air.'

'That's what Rose said too,' I said. 'After a while Daisy just stopped writing to her. Back then, Rose had no way of tracing her, but surely, with the internet, we should be able to find something out.'

'She couldn't just disappear,' said Kate.

'Maybe she took her aunt's name or something,' said Zoe.

'Or maybe she died,' whispered Kate.

'No way,' I said. 'She couldn't be dead. I know she's alive.'

'How do you know that?' asked Kate gently.

'I just know,' I said, even though that sounded totally stupid and pathetic. 'I know Daisy is alive. I know we can prove that her father was innocent, and then we can track her down and tell her the good news. It's going to happen – I've made up my mind.'

* * *

That night I looked at Daisy's photo for a long time. I don't usually talk to photographs of ancient people, but I couldn't stop myself.

'I'm going to help you Daisy,' I said. 'I'm going to find out what really happened. I'm going to make it right again. I promise.'

* * *

'Any bright ideas?' asked Kate when we met the next day.

'Nope. You?'

She shook her head. We sat on my garden wall for a long time, saying nothing.

'Do you ever watch *CSI*?' I asked in the end.

'Nope,' said Kate. I'd forgotten that she hardly ever watches TV. She prefers looking at stars and plants and stuff.

'Well,' I said. 'On *CSI*, when they're trying to solve a crime, they always try to find a motive.'

'And your point is?'

'Motives are crucial. If Jean-Marc didn't take the chalice that means George Eades was lying when he said he saw him do it. So we need to find out why he told that lie. We need to know what his motive was. That's the key to finding out the truth.'

'That makes perfect sense,' said Kate. 'Only trouble is, George Eades is probably dead by now, and I'm guessing his motive died with him.'

'There is one thing we could do,' I said. 'Maybe we could track down his family.'

Kate didn't say anything, but I was kind of warming up, so I didn't let that bother me.

'Maybe he has grandchildren who know what happened,' I said. 'Maybe they could tell us something that would help us.'

'What makes you think that?'

'Well, people know stuff about their grandparents don't they?'

She narrowed her eyes. 'What kind of stuff do you know about your grandparents?'

I giggled. 'I know that my granny loves toffees that come in a blue tin, even though she's afraid they will damage her false teeth. I know that my granddad says rude words under his breath when he can't solve the daily crossword.'

Kate laughed too. 'Exactly. All you know about your grandparents is useless stuff.'

'Well in the absence of a better idea, I still think we should talk to the Eades family, and see if they can help us.'

'But—'

'You know everyone around here, Kate. Are there any people called Eades still living in the neighbourhood?'

'Mmmm, yeah,' she said, not very enthusiastically. 'But I'm not sure that—'

'Where do they live?' I asked.

I jumped down from the wall, but Kate didn't move.

'Come on,' I said, getting excited. 'Why aren't you coming?'

'Well, you see—'

I grabbed her arm. 'Don't worry, Kate,' I said. 'I'll do all the talking if you want. You can just show me the way, and be there for moral support. I like doing this kind of thing.'

Kate looked like she was going to say something, and then she changed her mind. She gave a big shrug and a sigh.

'Whatever,' she said. 'No matter what I say, I know you're going to go ahead with this. We might as well just get it over with.'

I walked beside her as Kate slowly led the way towards the village. She didn't say anything, but

I was too excited to care.

'There,' she said finally, pointing at a small house. 'That's where the only Eades family I know lives, but—'

I knew that if I hesitated, Kate would find a reason to back out, so I opened the gate and marched up to the door of the house. As I knocked, Kate sidled up and stood beside me. She looked kind of edgy, like she was getting ready to make a quick escape.

I knocked again, and a second later the door was open and a stunning blonde girl was standing there in pyjamas.

'What do you two losers want?' she asked.

Cathy?

I opened my mouth, but no sound came out.

'It had better be good,' said Cathy. 'I'm totally exhausted. Do you have any idea how tiring the flight from Dubai is? Even in first class, it's totally impossible to get any sleep.'

I stood there like an idiot. How had we

ended up talking to Cathy – the meanest, most horrible bully in the history of the world? I looked at Kate, but her head was down, and she was examining her shoes like they contained the hidden secrets of the universe.

I remembered the summer when Kate and I first met. Back then, she was all weird and sullen and sad and lonely. Back then, Cathy had spent her time calling Kate names and being mean to her. (Back then, Lily used to be friends with Cathy, but luckily she started to hang out with Kate and me, and she got sense in the end.)

I couldn't stop staring at Cathy. Even though she claimed to be tired, she looked like she'd just walked out of a beauty salon. Her hair was perfect, and her pyjamas looked like something you could easily wear to the Oscars. I have to admit that people who look as perfect as that scare me a bit.

I knew this was a terrible mistake, and I was getting ready to walk away, but then I saw that

Kate wasn't moving. She looked cross and upset, but kind of determined too. She caught my eye and gave a small nod, which I guessed meant that she wanted me to continue – so I did.

'Er, hi Cathy,' I said. 'Kate and I would like to talk to you about one of your ancestors.'

Cathy's eyes opened wide, becoming even bigger and bluer and more amazing as they did so.

I kept talking. 'You see there's this girl called Daisy, well she's not a girl any more, she must be an ancient old lady by now, but she used to be a girl and she used to live in Seacove years and years ago, and …'

Cathy gave a pretty yawn, holding perfectly manicured fingers over her mouth. The sleeve of her pyjama top slipped down, so I got a good view of her golden, suntanned arm.

'Is this story actually going somewhere?' she said. 'Or are you just exercising your lungs? I'm just wondering, because unlike you, I actually have a life, and I'd like to get on with it.'

And then I knew that this was never, ever going to work. Even if she knew anything about George Eades, Cathy was too mean and horrible to share it with us. She'd just use it to taunt and annoy us.

'Oooops,' I said. 'Our bad. We seem to have called to the wrong house.'

Then I grabbed Kate's arm and we ran out the gate and down the road towards the beach.

'You knew, didn't you?' I asked, as soon as we were settled on our favourite spot in the sand. 'You knew Cathy was going to be there.'

Kate shrugged. 'I suspected, but I didn't know for certain sure. I know that Mrs Eades is Cathy's aunt, and that Cathy stays there a lot in the summer. And I'd heard a rumour that she was going to be back in town soon.'

'But why didn't you tell me?'

She didn't answer.

'Kate?' I said.

'I tried.'

I felt my face going red as I realized that this was true. She'd tried a few times, but I hadn't listened.

'But still you came with me,' I said. 'You stood outside that door, even though you knew there was a good chance that Catty Cathy was going to open it.'

'I know what it's like to have your family break up into little pieces,' said Kate. 'My mum and my dad both vanished out of my life when I was little, so I know exactly how Daisy must have felt. I wanted to help to make things right for her again.'

'You were prepared to face that evil bully, for Daisy's sake? That's totally brave and crazy.'

Now Kate's face turned red to match mine. She hates being the centre of attention.

'We should go back there,' she muttered. 'We should try again – for Daisy's sake.'

I shook my head. 'No way. That's not going

to happen. I want to help Daisy just as much as you do, but not if it means giving Cathy another chance to pick on us. We'll have to think of something else.'

'Like what?'

And how was I supposed to answer that?

* * *

'Great news,' said Zoe when we met her later. 'I've spent hours on the internet. I've managed to track Daisy down to a school in Chicago. She started attending there in January 1948.'

'So Daisy really made it to secondary school,' I sighed. 'That's so great. Maybe her dream of being a children's nurse came true after all.'

'Maybe,' said Zoe. 'But she left that school in 1950, and I can't find where she went next.'

'So is that the end of the trail?' asked Kate.

Zoe grinned. 'No way,' she said. 'I'm not giving up that easily. This research is really interesting. I'll find out what happened to your old friend – it might just take a bit of time, that's all. Now what about you girls? How did you get on today?'

So Kate and I told her all about Cathy and our failed attempt to get more information about George Eades.

Martha came in and heard what we were saying.

'You've got it all wrong, girls,' she said. 'That Eades family in the village are not related to old George Eades at all. They're blow-ins – they've only been around here for thirty-five years or so.'

We all laughed and Martha pretended to be offended.

'OMG,' I said, remembering how Cathy had looked at Kate and me like we were total losers. 'That's awful news. We totally embarrassed ourselves in front of Cathy, and it was all for nothing.'

'She must have thought we were complete

idiots,' said Kate helpfully.

I could feel my face going red at the thought of how I'd prattled on to Cathy. She usually bullied us for nothing. Now that we'd acted like weirdos in front of her, there was no telling what she was going to do.

'So where did George Eades live anyway?' I asked, changing the subject.

'He was from Kylebridge at the other side of the bay,' said Martha. 'But there's no point in going looking for him over there – unless you fancy visiting the graveyard. George Eades died donkey's years ago.'

'Did he have a family?' asked Kate, who was looking a lot more enthusiastic now that Cathy was out of the picture.

'I don't know who's left now,' said Martha. 'I haven't been to Kylebridge for years. But George had a couple of sons, so no doubt there's someone over there still.'

Kate looked at her watch.

'We could ...' she began.

'Don't even think about it, Kate' said Zoe. 'It's nearly tea-time. I know all this investigation stuff is exciting, but it's going to have to wait another day.'

'The Wicked Stepmother speaks,' said Kate, but she was laughing.

Zoe laughed too. 'If you don't behave yourself,' she said. 'The Wicked Stepmother won't make your favourite lemon cake for dessert.'

Then the two of them had a big long soppy hug.

I smiled. A year earlier, those two had never even heard of each other, and now they were the best of friends.

Life can be very strange sometimes.

Chapter Eleven

It was still early next morning when Kate and I headed off on our bikes. As we cycled through the village, I could see Cathy sitting on a wall outside the shop. She was with a girl I'd never seen before and they both looked like they were all dressed up for a party or something.

'Who's that with Cathy?' I whispered.

'That's her friend, Andrea,' whispered Kate. 'She sometimes stays with Cathy when she's in Seacove. She's kind of a mini-Cathy. She's not very nice.'

Just then Cathy looked up and saw us approaching. She pointed at Kate and said something to her friend. They both laughed – a mean, spiteful kind of laugh. Then Cathy held her nose, like something smelled bad.

I really couldn't understand what was going on. I know that bullying is always wrong, but back when Kate seemed weird, I could kind of understand why a mean girl like Cathy would pick on her. Now though, Kate was totally nice and normal, and still Cathy gave her a hard time. Clearly the whole bullying thing had always been more to do with Cathy than with Kate!

'Pay no attention, Kate,' I said. 'Cathy's not worth it.'

Kate didn't answer, but when I looked at her I could see a real hurt look on her face. Kate is my friend, and I hate when people upset her – so I knew it was time to do something.

I sped up my bike and zoomed towards Cathy and Andrea. When I got close to them, I suddenly veered to one side and cycled straight into a huge puddle of mucky water. It was totally brilliant – Cathy and Andrea were soaked from their perfect highlighted hair down to their perfect glittery red toenails. They jumped up from the wall and screeched and flapped at their clothes like demented chickens.

'Ooops, sorry, girls,' I said, without slowing down. 'I didn't see you there. I think your hairspray must have got in my eyes.'

When I was safely around the next bend, I stopped my bike. A second later, Kate stopped beside me.

'OMG,' said Kate. 'That was so cool, Eva. Did you see their faces? That's the funniest thing I've seen in hundreds of years.'

Then she looked at my clothes. 'But you're soaked too,' she said.

I grinned. 'I know,' I said. 'And I don't care. It was totally worth it. Now let's forget about Cathy and Andrea. You and I have got a job to do.'

★ ☆ ♥

Half an hour later we parked our bikes on a lane outside a huge old ivy-covered house.

'Here we are,' said Kate. 'This is the house Martha told us about. I bet all the answers we need are somewhere in here.'

I looked through the big metal gates. Suddenly I didn't feel so confident.

'Yeah,' I said, sarcastically. 'Maybe we can go inside and search the place. Maybe we'll look under a four-poster bed and find the stolen chalice with a note tied to the handle telling us who really took it.'

Kate rolled her eyes. 'Now you're just being pathetic,' she said. 'All we need to do is find someone who knew George Eades back in the day.'

'And then what?'

'And then we ask them a few questions.'

'But we can't just march in there, can we?'

'Why not?' asked Kate.

'And what will we say?'

'You'll think of something,' said Kate.

I liked her confidence in me, but wasn't sure that I deserved it. But we'd cycled a long way and it didn't seem right to give up without trying.

'Right,' I said, trying to sound brave. 'Let's go.'

I pulled one of the gates half open, and the two of us walked towards the house. Our feet made crunchy noises on the gravel, and that distracted me from the thump-thump noises my heart was making. I wasn't sure what exactly I was afraid of, and in a way, that made things even worse. I was tempted to turn around and run.

'If there's a guard dog, I'm totally out of here,' I said.

'This is important,' said Kate. 'We can't let Daisy down.'

'If there's a dog chewing my leg, we might

just have to let her down,' I muttered.

Kate laughed. She totally loves all animals, even scary ones with big sharp teeth.

After what felt like a hundred years, we made it safely to the front door.

'Maybe no one lives here any more,' I said.

'If that's the case, then someone should tell the milkman,' said Kate, pointing to a bottle of milk on the doorstep.

I knocked and gave a small jump as I heard the sound of the knock echoing through the house. A long minute passed.

'I don't think anyone's home,' I said, trying not to sound too relieved.

I was getting ready to walk away when we heard the click of high-heeled shoes on a wooden floor. I heard the sound of keys being turned, and seconds later, the door was open and a woman was standing looking at us.

'Yes?' she asked. 'What can I do for you two girls?'

The woman was smiling at us in a friendly kind of way, and I started to feel a small bit braver.

'Er, hi,' I said. 'My name is Eva, and this is my friend, Kate.'

The woman probably guessed that we hadn't walked up her driveway and knocked on her door just to tell her our names. She looked at my mucky clothes, and she seemed to be waiting for me to say something else. Only trouble was, I didn't know how to continue.

I looked desperately at Kate, but she just shrugged helplessly.

'Er ...... er ...... Kate and I cycled here from Seacove,' I said. 'Er ... we're really interested in local history ... it's kind of like our specialist subject ... and we ...... were wondering ... if ... if well if you happen to know anything about a man called George Eades.'

'Of course I know something about George Eades,' the woman said. 'He was my grandfather.

But he was a quiet, private man and I'm afraid I can't see why you girls would be interested in him.'

By now I was getting desperate. The vague plan I'd come up with in the safety of my own garden wasn't much help now that I was standing on this doorstep trying to make conversation with George Eades' grand-daughter.

I looked at Kate again, but she was no help whatsoever. She was playing with a piece of her hair, and acting like none of this had anything to do with her at all.

'Er… we just wanted to know what George Eades was like and stuff,' I said.

This was turning out to be a nightmare. The woman was tapping her foot on the shiny wooden floor and starting to look impatient. I guessed we had about thirty seconds before she told us to leave.

'Just tell her the truth,' said Kate, finally finding her voice.

I knew she was right. When you can't think of any good lies, the truth is probably the best way to go.

I took the photograph out of my pocket and held it towards the woman. She took it from me and looked at it for a minute.

'That's a sweet photograph,' she said. 'But I don't know these people. What have they got to do with me? What have they got to do with my grandfather?'

'That's a photo of the Lavelle family,' I said. 'Daisy, Florrie and Jean-Marc. They used to live over in Seacove – in the little house where I'm spending my summer holidays. They were a really happy family – at first. But then Mr Lavelle got sent to prison for something he didn't do. There was a court case and we think that George Eades, your grandfather—'

Now the woman's smile vanished. It was like a shutter had come down over her eyes, and she looked blank and cold.

'I think you two girls have wasted quite enough of my time,' she said. 'I don't know what you think you are doing, but it's time to stop right now. Go home and play computer games or whatever it is young people do nowadays. Go away and stop bothering innocent people.'

She was starting to close the door and I knew this was going to be my last chance.

'It's never too late to right a wrong,' I said. 'Jean-Marc died and Florrie died, but Daisy might still be alive. Don't you think she deserves to know the truth about her father? If you know something that could help her, don't you think—?'

But now the door was fully closed. 'Good-bye,' came the woman's voice from behind the thick wood. 'And if you ever come back here again, I will be calling the police.'

Then I heard the click-click of her heels as she walked away.

'At least we know where we stand,' I said, as

we walked back to our bikes. 'I like people who make themselves clear.'

'Yeah,' said Kate. 'But it definitely wasn't a wasted journey.'

'How do you mean?'

'Did you see the way that woman changed? She was all sweet and smiley until we mentioned the court case. That means she knows something. She definitely knows something.'

'Yeah,' I said. 'You're right. But you heard what she said. Short of torturing her, I can't think of a way to get her to share what she knows with us, can you?'

Kate shook her head. 'So that's it,' she said. 'This is the end. We did our best, but it's looking like poor Daisy, wherever she is, is never going to know what really happened.'

The cycle home seemed very long and full of steep hills.

Chapter Twelve

All that night I had terrible dreams about Daisy. She was sitting on the end of my bed, combing her long, curly hair, and crying big, fat, wet tears. 'Why won't anyone help me?' she kept saying. 'Why doesn't anyone care?'

Even in my dreams, where magic can happen, I didn't know how to answer her.

But the next morning there was a present-day problem waiting to be solved.

Kate called over and sat in our kitchen with her head in her hands. When Mum and Dad spoke to her, she just gave the shortest answer possible, and then looked away.

Luckily, Mum was used to this kind of behaviour. The year before, Kate had stayed with us while her social workers were trying to find her a foster family. Even though Kate is my friend, I have to admit that it was a very, very long few days.

Joey came in after a while, and I hoped that would make things easier. Kate and Joey have always got on really well.

'Hey, Kate,' he said.

'Hey, Joey,' she said, in a dead kind of voice.

'Have you heard the joke about the blunt pencil?' he asked. 'Oh never mind – there's no point!'

Kate didn't even smile. That's when I knew things were serious – Kate *always* laughs at Joey's jokes, even when they are totally unfunny. Usually she laughs extra hard at the very bad ones, because she feels sorry for him.

Mum gave me a questioning look, but I just

shrugged. I had no idea what was going on either.

'Poor Kate,' said Mum. 'You must be upset about Daisy. It's terrible the way things turned out for that unfortunate girl.'

Kate looked up. 'I *am* upset about Daisy, but that's not what's …'

'That's not what's …?' said Mum helping her along, but Kate had her most stubborn face on.

'Nothing,' she said. 'It's nothing.'

'Come on, Kate,' I said in the end. 'You and I need to talk. Let's go to Jeremy and you can tell me exactly what's on your mind.'

❤ ♡ ♔

'Please,' I said, as soon as we'd climbed up to our favourite branch on our favourite tree. 'Tell me what's wrong, Kate.'

She only hesitated for a second. 'It's Zoe,' she said. 'Her boss from London called last night and offered her her old job back.'

'OMG!' I said. 'That's awful. What did Zoe say?'

'She said she's going to think about it for a few weeks. And that's really, really bad news. That means she's seriously considering going back.'

'Oh, you poor thing.'

I wriggled closer to her. It's not easy to hug someone when you're clinging to a branch, halfway up a huge tree, but I did my best.

After a minute Kate pulled away. I could see the beginnings of tears in her eyes.

'What will I do?' she asked. 'What will I do if they all go away and leave me here?'

'That's not going to happen,' I said. 'I've got ages left before I have to go back home. We'll work something out, I promise.'

'Eva, you're the best,' she said, and I tried to smile as I wondered what on earth I was going to do to help her.

♔ ♚ ♜

The next few days were really weird. The weather changed, and it was too cold for the beach. Most days Kate and I just put on our fleeces and wandered around Seacove, bored.

Kate was in a constant bad mood, and nothing I could say or do would make her give more than a small, sad smile. She was turning into the sullen girl I had first known, and, even though this drove me crazy, I couldn't really blame her.

I was in kind of a bad mood myself. I like helping people, and in the past I've always managed to do that, but now everything seemed to be going wrong. I'd failed miserably in my efforts to help Daisy, and now that Kate needed me, I couldn't do anything for her either.

I was a failure. A big useless failure.

I began to wish that the holidays were over, so I could get back to my real life in town.

* * *

One day Kate and I walked in to the village to

get some shopping for my mum.

'It's Simon's second birthday soon,' said Kate. 'And Zoe's going to make a special cake for him. She said you can come for tea that evening if you like.'

I was glad to have something to look forward to, but kind of sad that a two-year-old's birthday was looking like it was going to be the highlight of my week. 'That'll be nice,' I said.

'I suppose,' said Kate, not looking convinced.

Suddenly I got angry at her. 'Come on, Kate,' I said. 'You have to snap out of it. Why do you always have to expect the worst?'

'What do you mean?'

'Maybe Zoe won't want to go back to London. Maybe she'll turn the job down and decide she wants to stay here.'

'Maybe she will,' said Kate. 'But then again maybe she won't. And then what will I do? I love having Dad and Zoe and Simon around. I've got used to having a proper family, Eva.

I've got used to being like everyone else. I don't want to go back to being a loser.'

'But that's pathetic,' I said. 'You've never been a loser, and you're not going to become one now – no matter what happens.'

She ignored me. 'And how am I expected to enjoy Simon's second birthday party, when there's a real chance I won't be around for his third or his fourth or his fifth? Oh, Eva, what if my little brother has to grow up without me there to teach him important stuff? What if he forgets me?'

And then she started to cry.

I stopped walking and hugged her for a long time. Then, while she was still sobbing loudly, I looked over her shoulder, and saw something terrible. It was Cathy and Andrea, walking towards us with big false smiles on their faces.

I pulled away from Kate, 'Quick,' I said. 'Wipe your eyes. Don't let them see that you're crying – they'll only use that to pick on you even more than usual.'

As they got closer, I could see that Cathy and Andrea were both wearing shiny green lip-gloss. Knowing them, it was probably the latest fashion, but it looked totally weird.

Kate was still wiping her eyes with the sleeve of her hoodie by the time the girls were next to us.

'Oh dear, Kate, you're crying!' said Cathy, in a sweet voice, almost like she cared. 'Is it because the hairdresser ruined your hair?'

Then she tossed her perfect blonde curls. 'Oh silly me,' she said. 'I forgot your hair always looks like that. You should try doing something different with it some time – like washing it.'

Then she and Andrea laughed, like that was the funniest thing they'd heard in hundreds of years.

I tried to think of a smart reply, but looking at Kate's sad face distracted me, and I couldn't think of a single word to say.

Now Andrea stepped forward. She touched Kate's shirt – a really cool one that Zoe had bought for her a few days earlier. 'That's lovely, Kate,' she said. 'It's amazing what a granny can do with a sewing machine and an old duvet cover.'

Kate pulled her arm away, but she said nothing, and that made me even madder.

I wondered if I'd get sent to jail if I punched Cathy and Andrea. For a second I wondered if it might even be worth it, just for the sensation of my knuckles crunching onto their ugly green lips.

Unfortunately though, I don't believe in violence, so I took Kate's arm and dragged her away towards the shop. At the last second, I looked back. 'Hey, girls,' I called. 'I like the green lips. Did you get them from snogging snails?'

But Cathy and Andrea were laughing at something else, and they didn't even hear me.

❧ ♡ xoxo

When we got back home I stopped at the gate of our house.

'I've got to bring the shopping in to Mum,' I said. 'Do you want to come in for a bit? Or we could go for a walk or something.'

Kate shook her head. 'No, thanks,' she said. 'I'm going to see if Zoe wants me to mind Simon for a while. I want to spend lots of time with him – so he won't forget me when he leaves,'

'If,' I said. 'If he leaves.'

But Kate was already gone.

Chapter Thirteen

A while later, Mum looked out the kitchen window towards the lane. 'That car is there again,' she said.

'What car?' I asked.

'That fancy big blue one. That's the third time I've seen it today. I'm beginning to think I should report it to Gerry the policeman. Whoever is lurking around can't be up to any good.'

I didn't look up from my book. Even in Seacove, a car in a lane isn't much to get excited about.

'Is there someone in the car?' I asked, not really caring either way.

'Yes,' said Mum, 'There's a woman sitting in the driver's seat. But I don't recognise her. I wonder if I should ...'

I knew she wasn't going to let it go, so I put my book down and walked towards the window.

'OMG,' I said. 'That's ......'

'That's who?' asked Mum, but I was too excited to answer her. I picked up my phone and texted Kate.

Come out – NOW!!!!

By the time I got outside, Kate was coming out of her front door. There was no time to talk. There was no time to plan what we were going to do.

We both walked towards the car. The driver, George Eades' granddaughter, had climbed out, and was standing staring at my house. She gave a small, embarrassed smile when she saw Kate and me.

'Oh, hello, girls,' she said.

'Hi,' said Kate and I together. I hadn't made

up my mind yet how friendly I was going to be, so I didn't say anything else.

'Is this the house where Daisy Lavelle used to live?' asked the woman.

I nodded, not sure what exactly was going on. This woman had made it clear that she didn't want to help us, so why had she suddenly shown up? Why was she poking around and asking questions about people she'd claimed to know nothing about?

It was like she could read my mind.

'Since you two girls came to see me, I've been thinking a lot about the Lavelle family,' she said. 'I can't manage to get them out of my mind.'

'You and me both,' I muttered.

The woman leaned against her car, almost like she needed all of her energy for what she was going to say next.

'My grandfather wasn't a bad man,' she said. 'But I'm afraid he did a very bad thing.'

Now Mum came out to see what was going

on. She doesn't like me talking to strangers – even ones with fancy clothes and big shiny cars.

'Everything OK here?' she asked.

'Everything's fine, Mum,' I said. 'This is …'

'Georgina Eades,' said the woman, holding her hand towards my mum. 'I've come to talk to your daughter and her friend. I hope you don't mind.'

'I think that depends on what you've got to say to them,' said Mum, stepping forward, ready to protect us if necessary.

'They came to see me the other day and they said something that made me think deeply,' said Georgina.

'And what exactly did they say?' asked Mum staring at me suspiciously, like she might not like the answer.

'They said, "It's never too late to right a wrong,"' said Georgina. 'And I have to agree with them. I think the time has come for me to tell them what I know.'

Kate looked at me with a huge smile on her face. Maybe the Daisy story wasn't over just yet.

In the end, we all went in to my place. Mum made tea for herself and Georgina, and I got glasses of milk for Kate and me. Then we all sat around the kitchen table and Georgina told us her story.

'I was brought up in England,' she began. 'And when I was young, I barely knew my grandfather – he was just a grouchy old man my parents took me to visit every now and again. But twenty years ago my grandfather became very ill and I came over here to live in his house and take care of him.'

'That was kind of you,' said Mum.

'Especially since he was so grouchy,' I added.

'Perhaps,' said Georgina. 'My parents had died by then, and George didn't have anyone else who could help him. I couldn't simply leave him to die alone.'

'So you moved in and got to know him?' I asked.

'Yes,' said Georgina. 'It was a difficult few months though. I'm afraid George was a bitter, troubled man. In the beginning, he would barely talk to me, but as the days went by and he became weaker, that changed. I think he knew that his time on earth was limited, and his conscience began to get the better of him.'

'And what about the Lavelles? What did George tell you about Jean-Marc? Why did he say he saw him stealing the chalice?' I asked impatiently, ignoring the cross looks my mum was shooting in my direction.

'My grandfather took many weeks to tell me this story,' said Georgina gently. 'I don't feel I can rush it all out to you in a few short minutes.'

'Sorry,' I whispered, feeling bad.

'My grandfather had two sons,' said Georgina.

'There was my father, Albert, and his younger brother Henry. Henry was always his dad's favourite. He was a handsome lad, and by all accounts, he was a real little charmer when he was a boy. Everybody loved him.'

I was wondering where this story was going, but one look at my mum's face told me that rushing Georgina's story was not a good idea.

'When my father left school, he got a steady job in the bank,' she continued. 'But Henry didn't want a settled life like that. He was an adventurer. Against his father's wishes, he joined the British Army. He went off to war.'

'The Second World War?' asked Mum.

Georgina nodded. 'Yes, and when he came back three years later, I'm afraid Henry was a different boy altogether.'

'Had he been wounded?' asked Kate.

'Not physically,' said Georgina. 'Physically he was as good as new, but the mental scars went very deep.'

'Did he have shell-shock?' I asked. 'We learned about that in history in school.'

'I think they called it something else by then,' said Georgina. 'But it was pretty much the same thing. It wasn't very well understood at the time, and, by all accounts, poor Henry suffered very badly. His hands shook all the time. He used to wake in the night screaming and roaring, and no one knew how to calm him.'

'The poor man,' said Kate. 'That must have been awful for his dad to watch.'

'I can only imagine,' said Georgina. 'His precious darling boy was changed beyond all recognition.'

'Did he get better?' I asked. Even though I had no idea how this story had anything to do with Jean-Marc Lavelle, I couldn't help being interested.

'I'm afraid he didn't get better,' said Georgina. 'As the months passed, things got even worse. Henry began to wander the roads at night, knocking on the doors of strange houses, and scaring people half to death.'

At last I began to get an inkling of where this story was going.

'And then one night, Henry came home with a big cut on his hand,' continued Georgina. 'George asked where he'd been, but couldn't get any sense out of him – Henry never remembered anything about his night-time rambles.'

'How awful,' said Mum.

'And the next day George heard that the church in Newtown had been ransacked, and that the valuable chalice had been stolen,' said Georgina.

'Henry did it?' I breathed. 'It was Henry who stole the chalice?'

Georgina sighed. 'The chalice has never been found, and we'll never know who took it. All I know is that George believed his son was guilty, and that was enough to set the terrible series of events into motion. George was terrified that his favourite child would be thrown into jail, and in his delicate emotional state, that would have been a tragedy.'

'So George made up the whole story about seeing Jean-Marc Lavelle coming out of the church carrying the chalice?' I said.

'So the police would stop investigating, before the trail led to Henry?' said Kate.

'And because George was respected in the neighbourhood, he knew people would believe him,' I said. 'Poor Jean-Marc never stood a chance.'

Georgina nodded and for a minute no one said anything.

'Don't judge my grandfather too harshly,' said Georgina in the end. 'Clearly, what he did was wrong, but you have to remember, he did it to save his own son. Parents will sometimes go to any lengths to protect their children.'

I looked at my mum, wondering how far she'd go to save me. She looked away, and I guessed she was thinking the same thing.

'I've got another question,' said Kate. 'Of all the people in the area, why did George pick on poor Daisy's dad? What did Jean-Marc ever do to George or to his son?'

'Was it just because Jean-Marc was French?' I asked.

'Well, yes and no,' said Georgina. 'My grandfather was a well-travelled man. He didn't have the same bad feelings towards outsiders that many people had in those days. But you're correct – he didn't pick Jean-Marc at random. He thought very carefully about it. He told me that he had hoped that Jean-Marc would just get a slap on the wrist from the judge. He thought that Jean-Marc and his family would be sent off to France to live. France is a wonderful country, so that wouldn't have been a tragedy.'

'I'm not sure France was so wonderful in 1947,' said Mum. 'It must have been a mess after the war.'

'And what about the life Jean-Marc had made for himself in Seacove?' asked Kate. 'Was he just supposed to walk away from that? Seacove is a wonderful place too, you know.'

'That's not the way things turned out anyway,' I said. 'Jean-Marc didn't get a chance to walk away from anything.'

'No,' said Georgina. 'George's plan was completely misguided. He lived an isolated life in his big house. He didn't understand how upset people were at the theft of the chalice. Unfortunately, by the time he realised that Jean-Marc was going to jail, things had gone too far, and George didn't know how to fix them.'

'He could have told the truth!' I said angrily. 'He could have made things right – it's never too late to do that, remember? If George had come forward and told the truth, Jean-Marc would have been released from prison. Florrie would never have ended up in the psychiatric hospital, and Daisy would never have been packed off to live in America.'

Georgina didn't answer. I could see her eyes becoming moist, and a small tear slipped down her cheek.

'I know,' she said. 'I know. What my grandfather did was very, very wrong.'

Suddenly my anger faded away. None of this was Georgina's fault, and it was brave of her to come here and tell her story.

Mum patted Georgina, like she was a little puppy. Georgina didn't seem to mind.

'So what happens next?' I asked. 'Are you going to tell your story to the police? And if you do, do you think they'll believe you? It's not like you have any evidence or anything. They might just think you're a crazy attention-seeking old lady.'

Now Georgina smiled. 'There's one important thing I didn't tell you yet. In his final days, my grandfather was even more agitated than before. The doctors said he should rest, but he couldn't lie still. He begged me to bring him paper and a pen. He wrote a statement, describing everything that I've just told you.'

'He wanted to make the wrong right,' breathed Kate.

'That was twenty years ago,' I said. 'What happened to the statement?'

'My grandfather gave it to me with very strict instructions,' said Georgina.

'Which were?' I asked.

'He made me promise to wait until he and Henry were dead, and then I should hand the statement to the police.'

'So why didn't the police do anything?' I asked. 'They can't just ignore stuff like that, can they?'

Georgina sighed. 'Henry is still alive. He became too difficult for George to manage, so he went to live in a veterans' hospital in England. His mind has gone now, but he is comfortable and well-cared for. He could live for many more years yet.'

'But that means ...' I began, but Georgina put up her hand to stop me.

'For the past number of years, I've complied with my grandfather's final wishes. I felt it was the correct thing to do. And I had made a promise of course, and no one likes to break a promise.'

'But......' said Kate, but Georgina kept talking.

'My grandfather never mentioned the existence of a daughter, you see, and I knew that Jean-Marc and his wife had died. I didn't see the sense in stirring up old ghosts. I didn't see how breaking my promise would help anyone.'

'But then Kate and I showed up,' I said.

'And told you about Daisy,' said Kate.

'Exactly,' said Georgina. 'After speaking to you the other day, I knew that what my grandfather had asked me to do was wrong. I knew I had to act immediately.'

By now Kate and I were practically jumping up and down on our chairs.

'So what did you do?' I asked.

Mum gave me another look, but I could tell she wasn't really cross. I could tell that she was dying to hear what happened too.

'Yesterday, I took George's statement to the main police station in town,' said Georgina. 'They are taking it very seriously indeed. I expect that they have already set the wheels in motion. I'm hoping that the serious wrong my grandfather did to that poor family can somehow be put right.'

My head was full of questions, but before I could ask any of them, Georgina stood up.

'I think I've taken up enough of your time,' she said. 'Thank you so much for the tea. It was very nice.'

She shook hands with everyone, and then she walked out of the room. A minute later we heard her car drive away.

Kate jumped up and hugged me.

'We did it, Eva,' she squealed. 'We really and truly did it.'

Chapter Fourteen

When Dad and Joey came back from their fishing trip that evening, Mum and I told them the whole story.

Dad hugged me. 'You clever girl,' he said.

'You're amazing, Eva!' said Joey.

It didn't seem right to argue with them.

'What's going to happen to Henry Eades now?' I asked. 'It's looking like he's the one who stole the chalice. Is he going to get into trouble for it?'

'I don't think so,' said Mum. 'It was so long ago, and most of the potential witnesses are probably dead. And since the chalice was never found, there's unlikely to be any new evidence.'

'And besides,' said Dad. 'Even if the chalice was found, and there was evidence pointing to Henry, he'd never be sent to jail for something that he did while he was suffering from a war-related trauma. Mental illness is better understood these days. The poor man would get help, not punishment.'

'So it's all good?' I asked.

They both smiled at me. 'Yes,' said Mum. 'There's probably a lot of paperwork to be done somewhere, but I figure that, before too long, Daisy's dad will get a posthumous pardon.'

'What's "posthumous"?' asked Joey. 'Is it something to do with possums? We learned about them in school – they are totally cool animals.'

'No,' said Dad, trying not to laugh. 'Posthumous means after death. I'm afraid a pardon won't be much good to poor old Jean-Marc, but if Daisy's still alive, I expect it will mean a lot to her.'

Just then the door burst open and Kate rushed in. 'Sorry for not knocking but something incredible has just happened,' she said in a rush. 'Zoe's found Daisy! How totally amazing is that?'

I followed Kate back to her place and Zoe told us the whole story.

'It was really frustrating me,' she said. 'Everywhere I looked for Daisy Lavelle, I came up against a blank wall. I was beginning to fear that she was gone forever. And then I decided to track down some of the girls who were at school in Chicago with her. After a while, I found one who was able to help me. She told me that Daisy got married very young.'

'And changed her surname – that's why we couldn't find her,' added Kate. 'Daisy Lavelle didn't exist any more.'

'I managed to access the Chicago marriage records,' continued Zoe. 'And this morning I isolated the right one. In 1953, Daisy Lavelle became Daisy Marcheson. Once I knew that, I was able to follow a trail.'

'And where did the trail lead to?' I asked.

'All kinds of places,' said Kate. 'It's like a very complicated treasure hunt.'

'After her marriage, Daisy went to college,' said Zoe.

'And?'

By now Kate was practically jumping up and down with excitement. 'And she qualified as a children's nurse in 1955,' she said. 'Isn't that the totally coolest thing ever?'

'So her dream came true in the end,' I said. 'That's so brilliant.'

'Daisy went on to have five children of her own,' said Zoe. 'Three girls and two boys. She and her family moved to California in the 1960s.'

'Lucky her,' sighed Kate's Dad.

Zoe rolled her eyes and went on. 'They lived in Santa Barbara for many years.'

'And is she still . . .?'

I didn't dare to finish my sentence, but Zoe knew what I meant.

'As far as I know,' she said. 'I found a recent photograph of her. It was taken at a hospital function for retired nurses and was published in the local paper.'

'When was this?' I asked weakly.

'Just a few weeks ago,' said Zoe. 'Look.'

I followed her to the computer and watched as a photograph popped up on the screen. It was a woman, holding a huge bunch of flowers, and smiling a big happy smile. The little girl with the curls was gone, but there was no mistaking the huge, dark eyes.

'OMG,' I sighed. 'It's really you, Daisy. At last we've found you.'

Kate's dad made us a big jug of lemonade, and the four of us sat around the table talking for a long time.

I was impatient.

'Can we find Daisy's phone number?' I asked. 'Can we ring her now? Does anyone know what time it is in California?'

Zoe smiled. 'Maybe we'd better move a bit more slowly,' she said.

I didn't agree. 'Daisy must be ancient by now,' I protested, too impatient to do the maths. 'While we're faffing around here, she might die or something. If we delay, she might never know the truth about why her dad ended up in jail.'

Kate's dad looked at the photo, which was still on the computer screen. 'She looks healthy enough to me,' he said. 'But you don't want to frighten her.'

'Or raise false hopes,' said Zoe.

'What do you mean by false hopes?' asked Kate.

'Well,' said Zoe. 'What Georgina told you about George's statement sounds promising, but we really don't know what's going to happen next. Someone somewhere has to do a lot of paperwork before this whole thing is sorted out properly.'

'So we sit here and do nothing?' I asked. 'I totally don't like the sound of that.'

Zoe laughed. 'No,' she said. 'After all these years, I don't think doing nothing is an option.'

'So let's give her a call,' I said. 'What are we waiting for?'

'Are you always this impatient, Eva?' asked Patrick.

I wondered if he was cross with me. I thought back to when I'd first met him in London. It was after he'd run away from Seacove, and from Kate. I said some fairly bad things to him then. It worked, and he came back, but I still felt kind of guilty when I was around him.

But then he laughed.

'It's OK,' he said. 'It doesn't matter if you're always like this. It seems to work wonders – and no one knows that as much as Kate and I do.'

He and Kate hugged then, and it was totally soppy, but totally sweet too. I felt sad though. What was the point of Kate and her dad getting on so well, if he was going to pack up and head off to London again with Zoe and Simon? Wasn't she going to just end up even sadder than before? And what kind of a result was that going to be?

Zoe interrupted my thoughts. 'How about I go to the police station in town tomorrow and make a few enquiries?' she said. 'Then, if it's really looking like Jean-Marc is going to be pardoned, I think it's best if we write to Daisy, and break the news to her gently. How does that sound?'

'It sounds like it's going to take ages and ages,'

I said, even though I kind of knew she was right.

Daisy had waited more than sixty years for justice, surely a few more days weren't going to hurt.

Chapter Fifteen

After that, things were kind of weird.

Zoe sprang into action and showed us how efficient she could be. She made tons of phone calls and had meetings with the police inspector and lots of officials and some of the local councillors. Finally, a few days later, she came home with a huge smile on her face.

'There are a few more formalities to tidy up,' she said. 'But basically, everything is sorted. Very soon, Jean-Marc is going to get the pardon he deserves.'

When Kate and I had finished dancing around the room, we helped Zoe to compose a letter to Daisy in California. Then the three of us walked to the post office together, wheeling Simon in his buggy.

'This is a very special moment, Simon,' Kate kept saying. 'This is where we change someone's life.'

Each time she said it, Simon made a loud raspberry sound with his lips and we all laughed.

That night I had a sleepover in Kate's place. When it got dark, her dad allowed us to lie in the garden for a while, looking at the stars. Kate lay there with a half-smile on her face. I thought back to all the times she and I had watched the same stars hanging in the same velvety blue sky.

Kate was really, really happy about Daisy, but that hadn't made her own problems go away. Soon Zoe was going to have to make a big decision – and when she did, she might just break Kate's heart.

I didn't want to spoil the moment, but I knew I had to ask.

'What do you think Zoe's going to decide about the job in London?'

'I think it's going to be OK,' said Kate. 'I don't think she's going to leave.'

'That's brilliant news!' I said. 'When did she tell you that?'

'Well, she didn't exactly tell me.'

'So why . . .?'

She turned to face me in the darkness. 'You helped Daisy. Even after all those years, you managed to make things right again.'

'It wasn't just me,' I said. 'It was you and Zoe, and Georgina and Rose and the librarian and—'

'It was mostly you,' said Kate. 'The rest of us were prepared to accept that Jean-Marc was guilty. If you hadn't believed in him, none of this would have happened.'

I was embarrassed and confused.

'Thanks – but what's this got to do with Zoe's job in London anyway?'

Kate smiled. 'You can do *anything*, Eva. You

saved Jeremy. You got Dad to move back here. You helped Daisy. You did all those things, so I know you can find a way to make Zoe stay. I just know it.'

I didn't say anything.

How could I explain?

Some things can't be fixed.

Sometimes, no matter what you do, there's not going to be a happy-ever-after.

But Kate had turned away again and was gazing up at the stars. 'Look, Eva,' she said. 'Do you remember what I taught you? There's Lyra, and over there is the Plough, and there's ...'

But I'd stopped listening.

How could I look up at the stars when there was a big problem right here on earth?

Next day, Kate was still in a good mood. That made me kind of nervous, but I didn't say anything. I didn't want her to slip back into being the sulky girl I was half-afraid of.

Mum made us a picnic and we set off for the beach. On the way, we met Cathy and Andrea. I braced myself for more insults – and I didn't have to wait long.

Cathy looked at our bag of food. 'Hope you've got lots to share with your imaginary friends from the past,' she said. 'By the way, how is that girl, Daisy or Violet, or whatever she was called? Has she made up her mind if she's a little girl or a wrinkly old hag?'

I ignored her and kept on walking. Then, as always, Cathy began to pick on Kate.

'That's a cool top you're wearing, Kate,' she said. 'I remember when that was in fashion. Three years ago, I think, or was it four?'

Then she and Andrea collapsed into fake loud laughing, while I pushed past them and kept walking towards the beach.

'I can't believe Lily used to be friends with Cathy,' I muttered. 'How could she?'

Kate shrugged. 'Lily got sense in the end, and that's the important thing. You shouldn't let Cathy get to you, Eva. I don't.'

But I knew she was only half telling the truth. Every time Cathy said something nasty to her, I could see Kate's shoulders hunch a little bit, and I knew she was just trying not to care.

'She says such horrible things about you,' I said. 'I wish there was a way we could teach her a lesson.'

'Calm down,' said Kate. 'She's not worth it. Now I'm starving. What did your mum put in those sandwiches?'

☼ ☾ ✿

We were just finishing our picnic when Joey and a few of his friends came and found us. 'You need to come home, Eva and Kate,' he said. 'There's people there and they want to talk to you.'

'Daisy?' asked Kate, looking at me.

'Couldn't be,' I said. 'The letter will barely have left the post office by now. Daisy doesn't know anything yet.'

'So who could it be?' asked Kate.

Joey shrugged and pulled at my arm. 'I don't know, do I? It's just a man and a woman. All I know is, Eva's mum said you're to come home – right this very minute – and don't delay – the lads and I have an important soccer game to play.'

Kate and I gathered up our things and followed the boys back to my place.

I peeped through the kitchen window and saw a man and a woman sitting inside. I knew I'd seen them before, but I couldn't remember where.

'It's the reporters from the local newspaper,' said Kate. 'They're the ones who wrote the story about you saving Jeremy.'

The man smiled at us when we walked in.

'Just in case you've forgotten, I'm Terry and

this is Karina. Your mother has said we can talk to you about Daisy Lavelle and her family.'

'Oh,' I said, embarrassed. 'It's no big deal. Kate and I were just trying to help.'

'Sounds like a bit more than that,' said Terry. 'We hear that you've uncovered a very interesting story, and we'd like to write about it for the weekend paper.'

So Kate and I sat down and took turns to tell the reporters the whole story.

'You two are turning into right little celebrities,' said Mum, when we were finished. 'Soon we'll have to stand in line for your autographs. I hope you don't end up getting big-headed.'

'These girls are far too nice for that,' said Terry, and I made a face at Mum, who made a totally weird and embarrassing one back at me.

Then, just when the reporters were about to leave, they turned around and came back into the kitchen.

'Do you two girls happen to be free tomorrow

afternoon?' asked Karina.

'Why?' asked Kate.

'We're looking for two girls to do some modelling as part of a summer campaign the newspaper is running,' she said. 'There's going to be a centre-page spread and we're also sponsoring posters that are going to be displayed locally. Would you be interested in taking part?'

'Tell us more,' I said, already picturing myself in some totally cool beach-wear.

So Karina told us everything that was involved – and the more she told us, the happier I got. This was almost too good to be true.

'It's an excellent cause,' Karina said in the end. 'And you'd be doing us a great favour if you'd agree to be part of it. The photographer and the outfits are all set up, but the original models dropped out at the last minute. If we can't find replacements, it's going to be very inconvenient for us.'

'That sounds like great fun, Eva,' said Kate.

'Let's do it.'

She looked surprised when I shook my head.

'But why not?' she said. 'It's not like we have any other plans for tomorrow.'

'I agree,' I said. 'It does sound like good fun. But the two of us shouldn't be greedy. We shouldn't hog all the attention around here.'

Now Kate was looking at me like I was crazy, but I ignored her.

I turned to Karina. 'Thanks for the offer,' I said. 'But Kate and I have to say no.'

Kate's face was red and angry. 'Hang on a sec,' she said. 'I think—' but I cut across her, and spoke to Terry and Karina.

'I think our friends Cathy and Andrea would like to take part in your modelling assignment,' I said. 'They're really good at that kind of thing. Will we get them to call to your office tomorrow afternoon?'

At last Kate understood what was going on. 'Cathy and Andrea would be just perfect for the job,' she said. 'Much better than Eva and me.'

'We'll trust you on that,' said Karina, who clearly had no idea what was happening. 'Tell your friends to be at my office by three, and we can start right away.'

'You're totally wicked, Eva,' said Kate as soon as the reporters were gone.

'I know,' I grinned. 'Isn't it great?'

Chapter Sixteen

It wasn't hard to find Cathy and Andrea who were sitting in their usual spot, fixing their hair and arranging their many jangly bracelets on their perfectly tanned arms.

Cathy looked at Kate's brightly-coloured top, and made a big show of putting her hands over her eyes. 'Oh, where are my sunglasses?' she said. 'Those colours are hurting my eyes.'

Even though I'd been practising insults in my room at night, as usual I couldn't think of any when I really needed one. For once, though, I didn't care.

Kate and I sat on the wall near the two girls and we launched into the conversation we'd rehearsed.

'I am soooo disappointed,' I said loudly. 'I always dreamed of being a model, and I thought this was going to be my big opportunity.'

'Never mind,' said Kate, just as loudly. 'It's not our fault. I guess they were looking for especially pretty girls for the photo shoot.'

When they heard the words 'photo shoot' Cathy and Andrea stopped pretending not to listen. They leaned closer to us, with their mouths open, like they were terrified of missing a single word.

'But having our picture on posters all over the place,' I wailed. 'That would have been so totally cool. I wonder what lucky girls they are going to choose as models instead of us?'

Now Cathy was practically licking her sparkly, pink-glossed lips. She did a little wriggly shimmy thing until she was sitting right next to us on the wall.

'I couldn't help overhearing your little

conversation,' she said, in a sweet voice. 'Who exactly is looking for models?'

I stared at her. 'Why should we tell you?'

She smiled a sickly smile, showing her perfect white teeth. 'Because I'm your friend, of course,' she said.

I thought of saying that if I had friends like Cathy, I would definitely never need enemies, but I bit my tongue. I couldn't risk spoiling the plan.

'Go on, Eva,' said Kate encouragingly. 'We're out of contention anyway, so we've got nothing to lose. You might as well tell them.'

So I smiled an equally sick smile back at Cathy, and began to talk.

'It's the local newspaper,' I said. 'They need two models. They're sponsoring a story in the paper and a charity poster campaign.'

'I simply love doing charity work,' simpered Cathy.

'Me too, I simply love it,' said Andrea,

sounding like a pathetic little parrot.

'When is this photo shoot happening?' asked Cathy.

'Tomorrow,' I said. 'If you go to the newspaper office tomorrow at three, the talent scout will decide if you have the look they want.'

At the words 'talent scout' Cathy looked like she was going to fall into a faint, like a princess in an old movie. She recovered quickly though. She jumped down from the wall and began to flap her arms madly in the air. I wondered if the jingling of bracelets had ever made anyone go deaf.

'I've got to get my hair done,' she said breathlessly. 'My highlights need freshening up.'

'I wonder if there's time to get a spray-tan done on my back,' said Andrea. 'I haven't had mine done for three weeks, and it's starting to fade.'

This was better than I could ever have imagined. I knew if I didn't leave, there was a real danger I was going to laugh in their faces. So, keeping my face as straight as I could manage, I grabbed Kate's arm, got up and walked towards the beach.

'Have fun girls,' I said. 'We'll try not to be too jealous.'

'Hope it's the start of a wonderful career for you both,' said Kate.

Then she whispered to me. 'Those two are always totally mean to us,' she said. 'Why would they ever believe that we'd help them?'

'That's the great thing about people like them,' I whispered. 'They're so busy being horrible, they don't have time to wonder if anyone is going to be horrible back. That makes them perfect bullies – and perfect victims when payback time comes around.'

And then, as soon as we were far enough away, Kate and I threw ourselves down on the sand and laughed until our faces hurt.

❀ ◎ ~

The next evening, Kate and I managed to walk right up to Cathy and Andrea without getting a single insult thrown at us. Both girls looked sulky and cross. Cathy's face was red, like she'd been scrubbing it for a long time.

'So how did the photo-shoot go?' I asked.

Neither Cathy nor Andrea answered.

'I can't wait till that special moment when I see the posters,' said Kate. 'Can you, Eva?'

'Barely,' I said. 'I'm sure that moment is going to be the highlight of the whole summer. At last you two girls are going to get the attention you deserve.'

And for once in their lives, Cathy and Andrea hadn't a single word to say.

~ ◎ ❀

Kate and I were lying in the sun in her garden the following day, when Patrick came back from the shop.

'I brought the paper,' he said. 'Who wants it first?'

'Oh, good,' said Martha, who was sitting in the shade of a tree nearby. 'I want to read the death notices.'

Kate rolled her eyes. 'Can we have a quick look first, Martha?' she said. 'We want to read about the Lavelles.'

Martha didn't object, so Kate and I took the paper and read the article.

'That's so cool,' I said. 'At last everyone in Seacove knows the truth. Jean-Marc's name has been cleared and all the people who thought badly of him will have to change their opinions.'

'Most of them are dead and buried, you know,' said Martha. But then she smiled at Kate and me. 'That's not the point is it though?' she said. 'You two girls did a great job, and you should be proud of yourselves.'

'Thanks,' I said, feeling suddenly shy.

I was just handing the paper to Martha, when I remembered, and pulled it back.

'OMG,' I said. 'We nearly forgot. There's something else we have to see in today's paper.'

I was so excited that my hands shook as I laid the paper on the grass and flicked to find the centre pages.

'Let's see,' said Kate, and I moved over to make room for her.

I turned one more page, and what I saw there was so brilliant, I hardly dared to believe it was true.

There was a huge black headline – 'Seacove Annual Anti-Litter Campaign'. Underneath the headline was a giant full-colour photo of Cathy and Andrea.

'OMG,' I said. 'It's even better than I imagined. It's totally hilarious,'

Kate made a funny snorting noise, and then collapsed onto her knees on the grass.

'I think I might actually die,' she said.

I knew how she felt, but I didn't want to die. I didn't want to waste a second of this magical moment. I gave a big sigh as I feasted my eyes on the picture.

Andrea was dressed up in a really weird owl costume. Her nose was covered with a huge pointy orange beak, and she was wearing a hat made of floppy brown feathers. She was holding a banner saying – 'Give a hoot, don't pollute.'

Even better though, was Cathy. She was dressed up as a burger, and it was hard to tell if she'd had time to get her highlights done, because none of her hair was visible. Her head was draped in gross red and brown lumps that were meant to look like mustard and ketchup. Her face was dotted with what I was guessing were meant to be sesame seeds, but instead looked like lots of dodgy blackheads. She looked like she wanted to thump someone – probably me for setting her up.

'OMG,' gasped Kate after a while. 'I can't

laugh any more. My head hurts, and my throat hurts and my sides hurt.'

'Not as much as Cathy's pride hurts, I'm guessing. What do you think, Kate? Result?'

She grinned. 'Definitely. Result.'

Chapter Seventeen

The next day Lily came back from her holidays.

'So what's been happening while I was away?' she asked when we'd all finished hugging.

Kate and I told her all about Daisy and the diary, and Georgina and the pardon and everything.

'Wow,' she said when we were finished, and before she could say anything else, Kate and I launched into the story of Cathy and Andrea and the photo shoot.

Lily had to wipe away tears of laughter as I described the picture in the newspaper.

'You should have seen their faces the next day,' I said.

'I know I was friends with Cathy before,' said Lily. 'But I've seen the way she talks to you, Kate, and she totally deserved what you did to her. That was such a brilliant idea. It sounds like you two have been having an amazing holiday.'

I looked at Kate. She hadn't mentioned that Zoe was thinking about going back to London, so I knew I couldn't say it either.

'So what are your plans, Lily?' I asked.

Lily sighed. 'Mum's business is crazy busy for the next few weeks, so I'm going to have to spend a lot of time helping her.'

'That's a pain for you,' I said. 'But great for your mum. She's really worked hard to get that business going, hasn't she?'

Lily sighed an even bigger sigh. 'Yeah, but Mum gets totally stressed when she's got too much work to do. And trust me, when my mum is stressed she is not fun to be around. I'll escape as often as I can.'

'Oh, I forgot,' said Kate. 'You'll have to escape tomorrow. It's Simon's birthday and Zoe's making a special cake to celebrate. She says you can come over if you want.'

'Brilliant,' said Lily, rolling her eyes. 'I'll talk to my manic boss and see if I can arrange to get thirty seconds off.'

While she was talking, the beginnings of an idea were coming to me.

'You should get your mum to drop you over to Kate's place tomorrow,' I said.

Lily made a face. 'There's no way she'll do that. She'll go all sarcastic and ask if my legs have fallen off and when I say no, she'll just tell me to use them to walk over to Kate's.'

'But your mum has to bring you,' I protested. 'It's really important.'

'Why?' asked Kate and Lily together.

I hesitated. It was too soon to tell them what I was really thinking. 'Er ... because I heard Zoe telling Martha that she hasn't seen your mum for ages, and it's time they met up for a good chat,' I said.

'Even though Zoe and Lily's mum have never met?' asked Kate with raised eyebrows.

I sighed. 'That's just a minor detail. Trust me, girls, won't you? And do what I say?'

Kate and Lily looked at me like I was an idiot, but neither of them argued, which was a fairly good start. I decided to continue while they were half on my side.

'Lily, you get your mum to drop you over tomorrow, OK?' I said.

Lily nodded and I turned to Kate. 'And you make sure that Zoe comes to the door and asks Lily's mum in for a cup of tea.'

Kate nodded too and I smiled. 'I'm glad that's all settled. Now who's coming for a swim?'

I was already in Kate's place the next afternoon

when the doorbell rang. While Kate and Zoe went together to answer the door, I took Simon in my arms, and tried to stop him from stuffing my hair into his mouth. (Eating hair is totally gross anyway, but since Simon's mouth was full of mashed banana and yoghurt at the time, gross wasn't a big enough word to describe what could have happened.)

When Kate and Zoe came back, Lily and her mum, Roma, were with them. Zoe and Roma looked kind of embarrassed, the way adults do when they've let their kids bully them into something.

We all sat around the table and for a while everyone made small talk, mixed up with lots of weird, long silences. Roma admired Simon, and the curtains, and the bunch of wildflowers on the windowsill. Zoe admired Roma's blouse and her hair. Everyone looked like they'd much rather be somewhere else.

My plan was turning into a total disaster, and

I didn't know how to save it.

In the end, Roma stood up.

'It's been lovely,' she said so convincingly that I almost believed her. 'But I'm afraid I have to go. I'm catering a fortieth birthday party tomorrow, and I have lots to do. I should be finished the cake by now, but I've been so busy, I haven't even started it yet.'

I was beginning to wonder if my plan had been totally pathetic, when Zoe jumped up from her seat too.

'Speaking of cake,' she said. 'Why don't I bring in the one I made for Simon's birthday?'

'Cake!' said Simon, and we all laughed a much-too-grateful laugh.

When Zoe arrived in with the cake, there was another silence – a nicer one.

'OMG,' said Lily in the end. 'That has to be the most amazing cake in the whole wide world.'

She was right. Zoe's cakes were always totally

cool, but this one was the best I'd ever, ever seen. It was covered in blue icing, and shaped like a toy-box. The lid of the box was half open, and all kinds of toys were tumbling out. There was even a perfect miniature copy of Simon's favourite toy duck.

Roma put on her glasses and gazed at the cake for ages – almost like it was a work of art that should be in a fancy gallery somewhere.

'You made that?' she said in the end.

Zoe laughed. 'Guilty as charged.'

'So you're a professional baker?' asked Roma.

'Absolutely not,' said Zoe. 'It's just a hobby.'

Roma touched the miniature duck. 'How did you make its beak?' she asked.

And after that there was no stopping them. They moved from Zoe explaining how to make the duck, to Roma asking her to help her with the cake for the fortieth birthday party, to Zoe agreeing to make all of the celebration cakes Roma needed. Then, when it was looking like things couldn't get any better, Roma told Zoe how she was struggling to keep her paperwork up to date.

'I know exactly how to help you,' said Zoe. 'My boss in London always struggled with that kind of thing too, but I found a perfect software package, and it made everything so much easier. I'll show you if you like.'

Roma didn't argue, and soon the two of them were sitting at the computer, and Zoe was explaining how to file orders, and keep track of costs, and profits and all kinds of totally boring stuff like that.

'Looks like we're not needed here any more,' said Kate, grinning. So the three of us took Simon for a long walk, and when we got back, Zoe and Roma were still chatting like they'd known each other all their lives.

The next day, Kate, Lily and I watched as a

truck pulled up outside the local shop. Two men climbed out and carried two ladders from the back of the truck. They propped the ladders up against the big advertising space near the shop, and began to pull down the faded old ad for the local newspaper.

'OMG,' said Kate. 'Are you thinking what I'm thinking?'

I giggled. 'If you're thinking that these nice men are getting ready to put up an anti-litter poster featuring our two "friends" Cathy and Andrea, well yes, I am thinking what you're thinking.'

We watched in silence, as the men used sweeping brushes to cover the whole billboard with paste. Then they took two huge rolls of paper from the truck, and stuck them to the board. No one said anything as the photo of Cathy and Andrea dressed up as an owl and a burger, appeared, bigger than life size, at the most popular spot in the whole village.

I found my voice first. 'It's brilliant,' I said. '*Everyone* is going to see that poster.'

'Actually it's kind of cool,' said Kate. 'I love dressing up. I wouldn't mind being in that poster – especially since it's for a good cause.'

'Me neither,' said Lily.

'And me neither,' I said. 'But that's not the point. The three of us have a sense of humour. We know how to laugh at ourselves. Cathy and Andrea just see this as a public humiliation – that's why it's so fantastic.'

'Don't you feel a tiny bit sorry for them?' asked Kate.

I felt like hugging her. Even after all the horrible things Cathy and Andrea had said about her, she still didn't hate them. I realised once again what a nice person she is.

'OK,' I conceded. 'I do feel a tiny bit sorry for them – but not enough to let it spoil this moment. Andrea and Cathy will get over it – and maybe they'll learn a lesson too.'

'What lesson will they learn?' asked Lily, and Kate grinned at her.

'A very valuable lesson,' she said. 'Never mess with Eva Gordon.'

Chapter Eighteen

As we got close to Kate's place, we saw a man walking along the lane in front of us.

'It's Miley,' said Kate.

I slowed down immediately. Miley was a local farmer, and even though he'd helped us to save Jeremy, I was kind of scared of him. (I'm funny that way – men with wild hair who carry big sticks and shout a lot always make me nervous.)

'I wonder what he's doing here?' said Kate.

Miley must have heard her voice, as he stopped walking and turned around to face us.

He shook his stick in the air, and I couldn't tell if he was waving at us or threatening to kill us.

'Hey, Miley,' said Kate. 'How are things?'

He smiled, showing us a big mouthful of brown and yellow teeth.

'I read about you girls in the newspaper,' he said. 'And how you solved that old crime about the chalice. You're very clever aren't you? Very clever indeed.'

'Maybe he wants your autograph,' whispered Lily, and that set me off in a fit of nervous giggles.

'Er, thanks, Miley,' said Kate.

Miley stepped closer. 'I can be clever too, you know,' he said.

I wondered, since he was so clever, why he couldn't find a belt to hold up his trousers, instead of an old knotty piece of string. But then I felt mean, as Kate smiled kindly at him, while we waited for him to say more.

'About twenty years ago, one of my lambs got lost,' he said. 'It took me two whole days to find her. She'd gone and rambled far away, right into the next parish and then didn't she fall into a ditch and get stuck.'

I resisted the temptation to look at my watch. My holiday was nearly over, and I didn't want to waste a second of it listening to a crazy old farmer telling us a boring, twenty-year-old story about a lost lamb in a ditch.

'Myself and the wife had to make a sling out of old rope,' he continued. 'And in the end we managed to pull the poor creature out. She was as good as new, despite her ordeal. That's the lamb, I mean, not the wife. The wife pulled a muscle in her shoulder and she went on about it for months until I had a pain in my head from listening to her.'

'Er, that's a really interesting story,' said Kate, and she stepped forward, and tried to walk past him. Miley waved his stick at her.

'Don't go,' he said. 'I'm not finished yet.'

Kate stepped back again, and Miley went on. 'As soon as the lamb ran off, I saw something in the ditch. It was like an old tin bowl or something.'

I held my breath. Could this story be going where I thought it was going? I looked at Kate, and her face told me she was thinking exactly the same thing as I was.

'So I pulled it out,' said Miley. 'And I sez to the wife, that might be handy for feeding the dogs or something. So we took it back to the barn.'

'And where is it now?' I asked.

Clearly Miley was enjoying his story, and he didn't let me rush him.

'For a few years, the dogs ate out of it.'

'And then?' asked Kate.

'And then it was thrown at the back of the barn for another few years.'

'And then?' I asked, half-afraid to hear the answer.

'And then it ended up in the old hen-house. One of the white bantams liked to sleep in it.'

'And then what happened?' asked Kate.

'The white bantam died last year,' said Miley. 'The wife was very sad about that. She was her little pet, you see.'

'And the bowl?' I prompted.

'I read about the lost chalice in the paper,' said Miley. 'And I sez to the wife, I wonder could that old thing in the hen-house be a chalice? And she sez, maybe it could and all, and I ....'

'And where is it now?' I asked.

Miley put down his stick, and for the first time I noticed that he was also carrying a dirty old sack. He took two corners of the sack and shook it, and something very old and dirty tumbled out.

No one said anything for a long time. I gazed at the thing lying on the grass in front of me.

Could this battered old object have been the cause of all the scandal in the area in 1947?

Could it have ruined the lives of the whole Lavelle family?

And then Kate was running madly towards her house. 'Don't go anywhere,' she called. 'Zoe printed out a picture.'

A second later she was back with a picture. She held it next to the thing on the ground, and we all looked at it doubtfully. The picture showed a shiny, perfect chalice. The thing on the ground looked like a piece of worthless old junk.

Then Miley spat on the cuff of his coat. He bent down and started to rub. After a minute, in the middle of the dull brown surface, a patch of silver began to shine.

'Well,' said Miley proudly. 'What do you think of that?'

'OMG!' I said. 'You've found the Newtown chalice.'

✿ ★ ☆

A few days later, it was time for me to leave Seacove once again. As soon as the house was scrubbed clean, and the car was packed up, Mum turned to me.

'Ten more minutes, Eva,' she said. 'And then we have to leave, if we want to miss the traffic.'

I knew the drill from previous years. I raced across to Kate's place.

Her Dad came to the door, and held Simon out for me to kiss. Simon is totally cute, but kissing a cheek crusted with dried-in porridge isn't exactly my idea of fun, so I gave him a high-five instead. He didn't seem to mind.

Kate came to the door then, and her dad took Simon inside. Kate was almost bouncing up and down with excitement.

'Zoe made the call last night,' she said.

'What call?' I asked, even though I was fairly sure I could guess the answer.

'The call to her boss in London. She told her she's definitely not coming back. She's going to stay here. Everyone's going to stay here in Seacove.'

I hugged her. 'That's so brilliant,' I said. 'Where is Zoe? I'd like to say goodbye.'

Kate grinned. 'She's not here. She had to go to meet Roma. They're drawing up a partnership agreement. They've agreed to run the catering company between them. And after they've drawn up the agreement, they're going to the printers to get flyers and stuff made.'

'Cool,' I said. 'And if they need models for the flyers, have they got Cathy and Andrea's numbers?'

We both laughed for a bit at the thought of Cathy and Andrea dressed up as sandwiches or cocktail sausages or something.

Then Kate got serious again.

'It's all because of you, Eva. You're the one who had the genius idea of getting Zoe and Roma together. How did you know they'd get on so well? Did you know they'd end up working together?'

I shrugged. 'Know is a big word,' I said. 'I

sort of hoped it would work out, and luckily it did. I just put Roma and Zoe together, and they figured the rest out for themselves. It wasn't exactly rocket science.'

'Maybe not,' said Kate. 'But it's still the best thing that's happened to me. I love Zoe so much. She's almost like a mum to me – except she's never embarrassing, the way mums seem to be.'

I smiled to myself, glad that Kate had never heard about Zoe's 'singing' in Jacob's pub.

'And things worked out for Daisy too,' sighed Kate. 'I really, really hope she hurries up and writes back to us. The postman thinks I'm stalking him the way I race outside every time I hear his van coming along the lane.'

'Well, you must promise to ring me the minute you hear a single word, OK?' I said. 'I don't want to be left out, just because I'm not in Seacove.'

She nodded. 'I promise.'

Then I checked my watch. 'I have to go,' I said. 'Mum and Dad will be waiting for me.'

'Oh, I nearly forgot,' said Kate. 'Zoe's really sorry she couldn't be here to say goodbye, so she left something for you.'

She ran back into the house and came out a second later carrying a cake. She put it on the wall near the front door, so I could look at it properly.

It was totally, totally amazing. On the top was a figure of Superwoman, but instead of Superwoman's face, Zoe had stuck on a photo of me. All around the edge, it said "SUPER EVA" in huge silver letters.

'That's so gorgeous,' I said. 'I don't think I'd ever dare to eat it.'

'You'd better,' said Kate, 'or else my Wicked Stepmother will hunt you down and kill you or turn you into a weasel or something.'

I giggled. Then I heard the sound of car doors slamming and the revving of an engine. I hugged

Kate again, and then I picked up the cake and walked away. I found space on the back window for the cake, then I jumped into the car, and dad started the engine.

And that was the end of another amazing holiday in Seacove.

Chapter Nineteen

It was a dull, chilly October afternoon when Mum drove me back to Seacove. The beach was deserted except for a man walking his dog. The sea was grey and choppy.

Outside the shop, the brightly-coloured buckets and shovels that usually hung there had been replaced by stacks of logs and bags of coal.

'It's all different,' I wailed to Mum. 'And I'm not sure I like it.'

Then I saw the notice-board on the wall outside the shop. It was a bit tattered and faded, but the picture of Cathy and Andrea was still there.

I giggled. 'OK. So maybe some things are still the same.'

Mum rolled her eyes and continued to drive.

✯ ♥ ♡

Kate came racing out of her house when she heard our car.

'You're here, you're here!' she repeated over and over, like a crazy girl.

'Who cares about me?' I said. 'What about Daisy? Is she here yet?'

'She had an unexpected stop in Dublin,' said Kate. 'So she won't be here for another few hours.'

I couldn't help feeling a small bit relieved. This was all kind of weird for me. Reading Daisy's diary and proving that her dad was innocent was fine, but the thought of actually meeting her was making me nervous. In my mind, she was still a young girl like me, even though I knew she was old enough to be my granny.

What were we going to talk about?

Knitting?

Arthritis?

The best place to buy big beige knickers?

Would she even know what a mobile phone or a computer was?

Kate brought me inside to her place. Her dad and Zoe and Martha hugged me, and Simon gave me a sloppy baby kiss. When no one was looking, I wiped my face with the sleeve of my jumper – baby drool on my face so isn't my idea of a cool look.

'We met Georgina Eades last week,' said Kate.

'How come?' I asked.

'She paid for the restoration of the chalice,' said Zoe. 'And there was a ceremony in the church, in honour of its return to its rightful home.'

'After a few decades in a hen-house,' said Kate, trying not to laugh.

We sat around the kitchen table. For the

first time, I noticed that Zoe and Kate were all bright-eyed and edgy. They kept looking at each other and grinning like they had a big secret they were bursting to share.

'What?' I said in the end.

'There's something I haven't told you,' said Kate. 'Zoe and I only found out last week, so we decided to wait until you got here to surprise you.'

'What is it?' I asked.

Zoe and Kate looked at each other and smiled again, but neither of them answered my question.

'Have you got Daisy's diary with you?' asked Kate instead.

'Of course I have,' I said, pulling it out of my bag. 'I'm going to give it back to her when I see her. But why do you need that now? You've seen it heaps of times already.'

Kate didn't say a word as she took the diary from my hand.

'I don't know how we never noticed it before,' she said, as she began to flip through the pages. 'It was staring us right in the eye, and yet none of us ever copped on.'

'Copped on to what?' I asked. I was getting fed up of the way everyone was being so secretive. Secrets are only fun when you're the one who knows what's going on.

'Patience, Eva,' said Mum, which was a bit mean, because I could see that she was dying to know too.

At last Kate found the page she wanted. 'Listen to this,' she said, as she began to read.

Dear Diary.

Mammy cries all the time now. I try to cheer her up but nothing works. She used to be so proud of her glossy hair and her trim figure, but now she doesn't care about anything. She sits at the kitchen table and drinks tea and eats so much bread that she's getting fat. Some days she doesn't get up out of bed at all. I don't know what is going to happen to her. I don't know what is going to happen to me.

'I read that months ago,' I said, as I put the diary back into my bag. 'And I still don't know where this is going.'

Then, when I saw Mum smiling knowingly, I began to get angry.

'Just get on with it and tell me, Kate,' I said. 'I totally hate guessing games.'

Kate just smiled, and if I was a violent person, that's when I would have thumped her.

'Daisy's mum's trim figure is gone, and she's getting fat,' said Mum to Zoe, ignoring me. 'Does that mean what I think it means?'

Zoe nodded and at last I understood.

'OMG,' I said. 'Daisy's mum was expecting a baby?'

'Yes,' said Kate. 'She was born a few months after Daisy left for America.'

'That's amazing,' I said. 'How did you find out? And how come no one around here seemed to know anything about it? What happened?'

'After you left Seacove at the end of the summer,' said Zoe. 'I wanted to know more about the Lavelle family. There were still a few unanswered questions, and they were really annoying me.'

'You wouldn't like Zoe when she's annoyed,' said Kate, and ducked as Zoe pretended to hit her.

'Anyway,' said Zoe. 'Before I was rudely interrupted, I was going to say that I managed to track down the records about Daisy's mum's time in hospital. They made very sad reading, I'm afraid. A hospital like that was not a fun place to be in 1947.'

'But the baby?' I said impatiently.

'It was a little girl,' said Zoe. 'Despite everything that had happened, she was strong and healthy.'

'The baby sister that Daisy had always

dreamed of,' I sighed. 'She must have been so happy when she heard.'

'I'm sure she would have been,' said Zoe. 'Only trouble was, no one told her.'

'I don't get it,' I said. 'Daisy had a right to know.'

Zoe sighed. 'Of course she did. But things were handled differently in those days. We don't think Jean-Marc was ever even told about his second little daughter.'

'And what happened to her?' I asked. 'Where did the baby go?'

'Daisy's mum was too sick to take care of her,' said Zoe.

'So when she was only a day old, the hospital people took her away from her mother,' said Kate.

'That's awful,' I said. 'Where did they take her to?'

'She was brought to Dublin, and placed with a foster family,' said Zoe.

'And is she ...?' I was afraid to finish the question. Suddenly the health of this person, who I'd only just heard of, was very important to me.

'She's alive and well,' said Kate. 'Zoe tracked her down. Her name is Nell.'

'And did she know ...?'

'She hardly knew anything at all,' said Zoe. 'The records of that time were sketchy, to say the least. When Nell went searching some years ago, she discovered that her birth parents were dead. But until last week, she believed that she was an only child.'

'That's so amazing,' I gasped. 'What a lovely surprise she must have got when she heard about Daisy. Have they met yet?'

'Daisy flew into Dublin last night and they were re-united,' said Zoe. 'After all those years, the two sisters finally met.'

'OMG,' was all I could say, so I repeated it over and over. 'OMG. OMG. OMG.'

♡ ♔ ♚

Half an hour later, I was so impatient I couldn't sit still.

'You're making me nervous, Eva,' said Zoe. 'Why don't you and Kate go for a walk or something?'

So Kate and I went to hang out with Jeremy for a while, and when we came back, Zoe had made mushroom soup for everyone.

'It's delicious,' said Mum.

'Dad and I picked the wild mushrooms,' said Kate proudly. 'We know all the best places to look.'

'I made up the recipe,' said Zoe. 'And I've been practising it for a dinner Roma and I are doing next week.'

Then she told us all about the plans she and Roma had for the business, and Simon sat on my knee, and I tried to stop him feeding me half-chewed soggy pieces of bread, and Kate's dad told pathetic jokes, and Kate grinned at me like a crazy thing, she was so happy with everything.

And then we heard the sound of a car outside.

'Daisy's here,' said Kate. 'She's really and truly here at last.'

Chapter Twenty

We all ran outside and watched as a car with two women inside pulled up in the lane between Kate's house and ours. As a woman stepped out of the driver's seat, I recognised Daisy from the photograph I'd seen on the internet. I gasped as I looked at the other woman and saw that, except for the fact that she was clearly younger, they could have been twins.

Daisy stood there for a second. She ignored the welcoming committee and gazed at her old home. I tried to see it through her eyes, and wondered how much it had changed. I thought of all the things that had happened since she'd last stepped through the front door. No one said anything, as tears began to well in Daisy's eyes, and drip down her wrinkled old cheeks.

Then, Simon, who was in his Dad's arms, leaned over and touched her face.

'Lady sad,' he said.

Daisy smiled, and for a fleeting second, I could see a glimpse of the young girl I knew from her family photo.

'No, darling,' she said. 'The lady isn't sad. She is very, very happy.'

After that, everything was easier. Martha stepped forward and introduced herself.

'Oh my,' said Daisy. 'Little Martha is all grown up!' Everyone laughed.

Martha introduced everyone else, and Daisy turned to the woman beside her, and stroked her arm.

'This is Nell,' she said. 'My … sister.'

She said the word 'sister' in a soft, breathy

kind of voice, almost like she couldn't believe that such a thing was really possible.

I looked at Simon and Kate. Simon was pulling her hair, and she was tickling his tummy to distract him. Suddenly I realized how very, very glad I was that Kate and Simon were going to grow up together. They weren't going to need a big reunion when they were old and grey. They were going to be best friends forever.

'Would you like to see the house?' asked Mum, who had brought Monica's keys with her.

'I would like that very much,' said Daisy, and we all trooped up the path.

Daisy guided Nell. 'Be careful here,' she said. 'There's a loose stone and it's easy to trip. And mind your shoes, it's rather mucky on this bit.'

'Oh dear,' said Nell. 'You've only been my big sister for a day, and already you're bossing me around.' Then they held hands for a minute, and gave each other soppy looks, like they had known each other all their lives.

I smiled. This was all easier and nicer than I had expected.

At first, Daisy seemed stiff and slow, but when she got to the stairs leading to what used to be her bedroom, she speeded up, and practically galloped up the steps. She almost ran to the window. She pulled back the lacy curtain and gazed out at the view that must once have been so familiar to her.

'It's all the same,' she said. 'It's all the same. Except … except … I expect to see Daddy working in the field, and Mammy hanging the washing on the line.'

Nell took her hand again and squeezed it tightly. I could feel tears coming to my eyes, as I gazed at the sisters. One had lost everything she loved, and the other had never even known that it existed.

'Why don't we let you two alone for a bit?' said Mum.

So the rest of us went back downstairs leaving

the sisters to share their sad and happy memories.

♔ ♚ ♛

Later we all went across to Kate's place. Roma and Lily showed up, and everyone settled down for tea. Once again, Zoe had made an amazing cake. All the edges were decorated with perfect yellow and white daisies, and it had 'Welcome home, Daisy & Nell' written on the top.

'This is far too perfect to eat,' said Daisy, but the rest of us ignored her as Zoe sliced the cake up, and it was gone in minutes.

While my mum tidied up the plates and cups, Daisy showed us the letter she'd got from the president's office, declaring that Jean-Marc was innocent.

'Daddy was right,' she said. 'Justice was done in the end. Such a pity it took so long.'

I'd have been really, really angry, but Daisy just looked sad.

'Are you bitter about all the people who

believed your father was guilty?' asked Zoe, getting straight to the point as usual. 'You and your mum and dad had such a hard time here – in this place where you'd thought you had friends – where people should have stood by you.'

Daisy didn't answer for a long time. Then she shook her head slowly. 'No,' she said. 'I'm not bitter. Being bitter wouldn't make me happy. My great aunt used to say that holding on to resentment is like drinking poison and expecting the other person to die.'

'Cool,' said Kate.

Daisy smiled at her. 'Things were different back then,' she said. 'People were secretive and superstitious. They weren't used to thinking for themselves. What happened to my family was very sad, but being bitter won't help me. I'll never forget, but I think I can forgive.'

Nell leaned over and squeezed her sister's hand, and everyone coughed and rubbed their faces and pretended not to have tears in their eyes.

After that, everyone chatted for a long time. Daisy told us a lot about her children, and her life in America. It all sounded strange and foreign, and very, very different to what her life would have been if she'd stayed in Seacove. It was totally weird how one lie from George Eades had made so much difference to so many people.

I hadn't noticed Kate's dad slipping away, and was surprised when I heard another car pulling up outside.

'Are we expecting someone else?' asked Kate.

Zoe just smiled at her, but didn't reply.

Then the door opened, and Kate's dad wheeled Rose into the room. Daisy was telling Nell all about her job as a children's nurse, and she didn't see her at first. Then she looked up, and her face went pale. I thought it must have been at the shock of seeing her friend all old and frail and in a wheelchair. That would have to be a big shock for anyone.

'Rose!' gasped Daisy. 'You're here. It's really you. And you haven't changed at all.'

She ran over and stroked her face, and hugged her, and they both laughed and cried and then laughed some more.

And all at once I realized that Daisy wasn't seeing the wheelchair or the wrinkles or the thin, scraggly grey hair. All she could see was her dear old friend from so many years ago.

❦ ❦ ❦

Daisy and Rose chatted for a long time. They told Nell all about Florrie and Jean-Marc. Then they told Kate and me about the many hours they spent in Manning's field.

'We call that field the Island of Dreams,' said Kate.

'How sweet,' said Rose.

'Mammy used to make us picnics,' said Daisy.

'We'd go off for hours,' said Rose. 'We'd lie on the grass and watch the clouds and talk about our foolish dreams.'

'And you climbed Jeremy?' I asked.

Rose and Daisy looked puzzled.

'The big tree,' I said. 'Kate and I call it Jeremy.'

I was starting to feel a bit stupid, but changed my mind when Daisy gave a big smile. 'Jeremy,' she said. 'A perfect name. I wish I'd thought of it myself.'

'We could bring you to Manning's field if you like,' said Kate. 'So you can see what it's like now.'

But Daisy sat back, suddenly looking old and tired. 'Maybe later,' she said.

'This must have been an exhausting few days for you,' said Mum.

Daisy smiled. 'Exhausting, but wonderful,' she said. 'Everything has been simply perfect.'

I saw my opportunity. 'There's just one more thing,' I said.

Everyone watched as I reached into my bag and pulled out the old, red, leather-bound book.

'I don't believe it,' said Daisy. 'It's my old diary. The one Mammy and Daddy gave me for my thirteenth birthday.'

I nodded.

'I thought it was gone forever,' sighed Daisy.

'Eva and I found it in the shed,' said Kate. 'That's what started this whole thing. That's how we knew about what had happened to your dad.'

Suddenly I felt embarrassed. 'I read it, Daisy,' I said. 'I'm sorry about that. I know that diaries are supposed to be private. It's just that …'

Daisy patted my hand. 'Don't apologise, child,' she said. 'I'm sure most of what's inside here is just girlish foolishness. And if you hadn't read the diary, none of us would be here now. Daddy would never have been exonerated, and I would never have found my lovely sister. I am so very happy that you read my diary.'

She took the diary, and for a long time no one said anything. We watched as Daisy turned the pages slowly, sometimes smiling and sometimes wiping away a small tear. Finally she got to the last entry. She looked at it for a while, and then she reached into her handbag and took out a pen. I held my breath as she turned to the next blank page. In perfect, familiar letters, she began to write.

October 22nd

Today, thanks to the kindness of strangers, I came back home.

The 'Eva' Series by Judi Curtin

Don't miss the other great books about Eva and her friends

Have you read them all?

Eva's Journey

Eva's Holiday

Leave it to Eva

Available from all good bookshops.

Eva Gordon is a bit of a princess ...

But when her dad loses his job and she has to move house and change schools, she realises things have changed forever. A chance visit to a fortune teller gives her the idea that doing good may help her to turn things back the way they were. Eva (with the help of best friend Victoria) starts to help everyone she can – whether they want it or not! And maybe being nice is helping Eva herself just as much ...

The story of
Eva's marvellous,
memorable summer!

Eva Gordon likes fashion, fun and hanging out with friends, so she can't believe she has to spend the entire summer in a cottage in the countryside with her parents.

Worse, it looks like she's going to be stuck with Kate, the girl next door who doesn't care about being cool ... But when the girls have to pull together to solve a problem, Eva finds out that there's more to life than having the right hair or clothes and sometimes 'weird' girls can make the best friends.

Fun, feisty Eva Gordon always tries to help her friends!

When Eva and her family head to Seacove for their summer holidays, she's looking forward to seeing Kate again, but it turns out things have gone very wrong for Kate. Her granny's in the hospital, and with no else to look after her, Kate's hiding out at home by herself, afraid she's going to be taken into care. Eva tries to be a good friend and help her out, but how long can a twelve-year-old manage by herself?

It's not just Kate who needs Eva's help, though helping Ruby turns out to be a LOT more fun!

Is there any way a trip away with Ruby can help everyone sort things out?

It seems impossible, but if you have a problem that needs solving, just leave it to Eva!

THE 'ALICE & MEGAN' SERIES
BY

HAVE YOU READ THEM ALL?

Don't miss all the great books about Alice & Megan:

Alice Next Door
Alice Again
Don't Ask Alice
Alice in the Middle
Bonjour Alice
Alice & Megan Forever
Alice to the Rescue
Alice & Megan's Cookbook

WHY NOT VISIT THE GREAT NEW 'ALICE & MEGAN' WEBSITE AT WWW.OBRIEN.IE/ALICEANDMEGAN

Latest Judi news, new books, events, free stuff!
Exclusive sneak peeks
'Ask Judi'
Great competitions and freebies
Reader Review – become an online reviewer ... and much more!

www.obrien.ie